The Gift Moves

The Gift Moves

STEVE LYON

LAUREL-LEAF BOOKS

Published by Laurel-Leaf
an imprint of Random House Children's Books
a division of Random House, Inc.
New York

This is a work of fiction. Names, characters, places, and
incidents either are the product of the author's imagination or are
used fictitiously. Any resemblance to actual persons, living or
dead, events, or locales is entirely coincidental.

Originally published in hardcover in the United States by Houghton
Mifflin Company, New York, in 2004. This edition published by
arrangement with Houghton Mifflin Company.

Laurel-Leaf and colophon are registered trademarks of
Random House, Inc.

www.randomhouse.com/teens

Educators and librarians, for a variety of teaching tools, visit us at
www.randomhouse.com/teachers
RL: 4.5
ISBN-13: 978-0-553-49494-5
ISBN-10: 0-553-49494-5
July 2006
Printed in the United States of America
10 9 8 7 6 5 4 3 2 1

For George Ella,
who said this sounded like
a story and not a song.

"The gift moves toward
the empty place."

— LEWIS HYDE
from The Gift: Imagination
and the Erotic Life of Property

Path

I would not cry. I left my family as the sun came over the mountain. We stood in the high pasture, where the trees were dull green in the dawn and the birds sang everywhere. I had gifts for everyone, everything I owned. When you leave that is what you do. My plate and bowl and cup I gave to my boy cousins. My knives and tools I gave to my uncle. My bed and blankets and tent I gave to his sister, and I gave all my clothes to my girl cousins. My warm hat and coat I gave to my father, Ram, who would give them to a cold cousin when winter came. He looked at the Sun and Moon pendant around my neck, which had been my mother's, wondering if I would give that, too. But I kept it.

My father touched my face as I turned to go. "Path. My daughter. Be happy in your work and your way," he said. The tattooed ram's horns on the sides of his head were yellow in the early-morning sun. I didn't trust myself to speak, so I nodded.

I left the dogs, giving each a bone, and left the sheep also. There was nothing I could give them, nothing they wanted but fresh pasture, and there was plenty of that along the South Fork of the New River. Woolly and warm, they pushed at me with their pointed faces and gave me their smell, rich and heavy far back in the nose. I would miss them.

And then I had given everything away but one last gift, and it was time to start down the mountain. I made my way down the path until I came to the New River and followed it to the loomhouse at the edge of the trees.

Bone and Blue Leaf were waiting for me, under the soft brown eaves over the front door. They had taught me all I knew of the cloth.

"A long journey you have," said Blue Leaf, "all the way to the ocean."

I looked back at her, still afraid I would cry if I spoke.

"So what will you find there?" she asked.

"You'll find hard work," said Bone, meaning Heron, known far and wide for her cloth. Heron who had taken me for a Hand, to work and learn for five years.

"You will find beauty," said Blue Leaf. "Heron will see to that."

Beauty. Which called to me in the cloth and yarn and dye. The pure thing I knew.

I opened my hand to give away my last gift, the shuttle they had made for me two years ago when I came to live with them. It was the last piece of the life I knew, and I put it in Blue Leaf's hand. "The gift moves," I said, somehow letting out the words and keeping in the tears.

"It moves," she replied.

Blue Leaf and Bone held up their hands and looked at me. I hoped they wouldn't try to touch me. I didn't know how to leave.

"Go now, Path," said Blue Leaf. "Go. Take with you what we have given you. Let it grow. Let it open wide."

And I couldn't stand it anymore. "Goodbye!" I shouted and jumped off the porch. I ran down the path by the South Fork of the New River, the Sun and Moon pendant swinging around my neck. I held it tight, and the tears stayed inside. The pendant, the clothes I wore, and my name were the only things I had left. And my tears, oh yes. Those I had kept for a long time.

My name, Path Down the Mountain, is tattooed on my body. It's a right-hand spiral of bright green footprints that start at the back of my neck and go over my shoulder, between my breasts, around my back and stomach, and then down my right leg to my big toe. It's a map, too, showing all the landmarks of the trail from our high pasture into the town of Boon. I had just passed them: the mountain, the pasture, the sheep, the rock, the forest, the river, the ruined bridge, the loomhouse, and now the Circle where I stood, green on the skin by my big toe, green as the grass under my feet. Even if I never walked this path on the ground again, I would carry it with me all my life and walk it as my name every day.

The Circle, all clipped grass and big enough to hold every one of the two thousand people who lived in and near Boon, was full of activity. People were carrying lumber, hammering, building all the stands and stalls for Midsummer Day. A pile of logs was stacked next to the fire pit in the center. In a month, on Midsummer Day, it would be crowded, the fire roaring, everyone there for the celebration that turns the year. But not me. I had not been to the fire since my mother brought me back to Boon.

Across the Circle the bus stood, waiting, eating grass. I walked to it, and it turned an eye toward me and rose. "Hello, Path," it said.

It put two of its twelve legs together to make a ramp and opened its door. I went inside and sat by the window. It was about half full, but I didn't recognize any of the other passengers. I was the only one to get on in Boon.

In a few minutes we began to move and soon left Boon behind. People got on and off the bus as it stopped and started again on the long slope to the flat land.

We stopped at a clearing in the woods and a family got on, mother and three children. They were dressed in bright clothes, and the children were jumping up and down, excited. I shrunk in my seat and hoped they wouldn't sit nearby. But they did, in the row of seats right behind me. They never stopped talking.

Some people just lay out their lives like so much cloth. You can't pass them by without stepping on it. And usually it's indifferent cloth. Poorly woven, the color muddy. But do they care? No.

Behind me the mother and her children unrolled bolt after bolt of talk, spread it on the floor, down the aisle, over the seats. And then they put down more over the top of that. I had to listen. First they talked about the bus. About how it was really alive, how it was made with termite genes and how it was part of a whole colony that had a queen and everything. Then they talked about their trip.

Like me, they were going to Rollydee. They talked about the big buildings they would see, the roads, and the crowds of people.

"Twenty thousand people," the mother said. "Living in one town. Can you imagine that?"

"No," said the children in a chorus, and then they started trying to imagine it by counting to twenty thousand on all their fingers and toes. When they ran out, they used their mother's, but that only got them to eighty.

A hand tapped my shoulder. I turned and saw a little boy, about five years old, with huge dark eyes.

"Can we use your hands?" he asked. "We need to count to twenty thousand."

The mother saved me. "Stop," she said and hauled him back into his seat. "You leave her alone. You'll just have to use your own fingers."

"I'm sorry," she said to me. "They're just so excited about this trip."

I let out a sigh of relief and turned back to the window. Outside, the forest slid past, endless and green. Like cloth, it had a pattern, a subtle one. Every so often the trees would line up in ragged rows, following roads that had been there once, too many years ago to count. When I saw that, I knew we were passing through an old town. These places had strange names. Winston-Salem. Maybe it had two names because it was two towns that grew together, like Rollydee, which used to be Raleigh-Durham. Greensboro. Burlington. Chapel Hill. Was there a hill there? A chapel, whatever that was? Once, these places were alive and standing, but now they were just lumpy spots on the landscape, overgrown with trees. People had taken all the building materials they could use, and time had done the rest.

Eventually the forest began to thin out. We saw more people and passed a couple of buses going the other way.

I knew we were close to Rollydee. And then, all at once, we were there. The bus stopped at the Circle, and I got out with everyone else, looking around. The buildings were as tall as I remembered and cast long shadows on the ground. People were everywhere. I thought how my mother must still live there, how I might walk around a corner and run right into her. But I knew it wouldn't happen. She probably wouldn't know me if it did.

I asked for directions to the train and was told to go straight across the Circle, walk two blocks down the large avenue, and I would come to the tracks. I picked up some fruit and cheese from a stand by the Circle and ate as I walked.

Ten or twelve people were waiting for the train, and no one knew when it would come. Trains are like that. They come in their own time, and when they come you get on. And you try to stay comfortable while you wait. When it got dark and there was still no train, an old man brought me a blanket.

"The gift moves, daughter," he said.

"It moves," I said and curled up by the tracks and fell asleep.

The train came at dawn, and we got on.

We traveled through land that got flatter and wetter by the hour. This was not like the bus. The train was fast and very small, just one car for people and one for freight. The track was flat and straight, and we stopped seven times. Each time, we had to get off and help load and unload freight.

By the last stop, everyone had got off except a barefoot man and me. When the train stopped at Dare Harbor, I asked the man how to find the boat to the Banks.

"Ah. Follow the track back a little ways, and you'll be there in no time. Look. You can see it from here."

He pointed, and I saw a small dock with flags and a little red boat tied to it. I ran there to find that the red boat was not mine.

"You must be Heron's new Hand," said an old man in the red boat.

"Yes, I am. My name is Path."

"And I am Last Wave."

"How will I find the boat that will take me to the Banks?"

"It's on its way now. They're expecting you, and they asked me to call on the radio when the train came in. Wait an hour or so, and the boat will be here."

I looked around. Dare Harbor was a tiny place. There was a dock where boats could come up next to the train and load and unload freight. I thought how some of the cloth I would make would come back there, to the dock and the train on its way to wherever it would go. I sat down to wait. The sky was hazy blue, and it was very hot.

I could smell the ocean, a strange new smell of fish and wind and salt.

Finally, after more than an hour, the boat came. I got on and soon had my first glimpse of the Banks.

From far off I could see little pieces of color poking out of the green above the white sand. As we got closer I could see more. I could pick out things and saw that there were different sorts of buildings. Some round, some square, and some with complicated shapes. I had never seen anything like that before, not even in Rollydee. And they were all the colors you could hope for, all next to each other in a bright jumble. You would never weave a piece of cloth like this, but on the ground it looked good. I could see the roof of a bright orange structure right next to a dome that looked like a giant robin's egg. As we pulled up to the dock, I could see that some of the buildings had pictures or words painted on them.

Heron was waiting for me. She looked just as she did when I had seen her in Boon half a year ago, when she picked me for a Hand. She was tall and slim, wearing a sky blue shift. Her hair was gray and tied in a knot on top of her head. The staff she carried was almost as tall as she was, and her face was set and proud. She looked old, like she had seen everything there was to see. She did not smile. Then her eyes found me.

"Path. I have been waiting. The boat is late and so you

are late. We have a long walk and little time before dark. Come now," she said and turned to go.

I had to scramble to catch up, and it was hard to walk on solid ground after an hour of riding in the moving boat. When I caught up to her, she sniffed.

"You smell like sheep, girl."

"Yes," I said. "I guess I do."

"Not for long," she answered.

The road curved inland and took us past the Circle. It was as big as the one at Boon, and it was full of people. They were building all sorts of things—sheds, tents, whole wooden buildings. I heard music and realized it came from radios that people had brought and set out on the grass. Heron walked into it and I followed.

"In a month it will be Midsummer Day, the day the year turns. The finest work we do will come out for this day and this day only. Do you think you have seen the best these hands can do?" She held out her hands to me. Long fingers, strong and rough. "You have seen nothing. Come here." She led me all the way to the fire pit at the center of the Circle. It was huge, more than a hundred feet across. "Look here," she said and pointed to a big wooden structure rising out of the pit. It seemed like a cross between a tower and a spring, a wooden spiral rising high into the air. "That is the fire pavilion for Midsummer Day. Every year we weave the finest cloth we can to cover it. It is beautiful. Glorious. And it is ours, ours for everyone to see."

* * *

We walked for a long time, with Heron swinging her staff and making me hurry to keep up. We passed people on the way: men, women, children, alone and in groups. Some pushed carts, and others carried things, talking and laughing. Dogs ran beside their owners, barking and running after each other. Everybody knew Heron. They would greet her, but in a distant sort of way, as if they knew they wouldn't get much of a response. And they didn't. Heron would nod, just barely, as they passed. She didn't introduce me to anyone.

We turned and walked along a path between two houses. By this time the sun was starting to go down and shadows were long, the light turning pink. The path turned into a sandy track, and we followed it up a little hill. The sand was warm and squished up between my toes, yielding beneath my feet. It was odd, like walking in something and not on it. A strange rhythmic sound was coming from the other side of the hill, a pounding and breathing. Then we came to the top of the hill, and I saw what made the sound. It was the ocean. Flat and blue all the way to the horizon. I felt exposed and small, with no mountains to protect me. The water kept coming up to the sand and falling down on it. Then it would pull back, rise up, and fall again. There was a strong wind, and it blew sand grains against me, so hard they stung.

"You came to learn the cloth, girl, did you not?" said Heron.

"Yes," I said.

"This is your first lesson, so learn now. What do you see?"

"The ocean," I said.

"The ocean. And it is vast. Get in it and you are in something big as the planet, with its own secrets and ways and its own will. Girl, that is how the cloth will be for you. As big as that. Each wave a pass of the shuttle through the web. You will find that the cloth, too, has its own way, its own will. Look. Watch the sea."

The waves kept moving, falling down, pulling back, falling again and again. I saw a small white bird with a black head fly straight into the water and come out with a fish in its beak. One tiny fish in the big ocean, but it was not safe from the bird.

Heron saw, too. "And learn this," she said. "The sea is not forgiving. Nor is the cloth. Nor am I."

We stood in silence for a few minutes. Then she spoke.

"Come, girl. We still have a ways to go." We turned and left.

Finally, when it was almost dark, we reached the Weavers' Yard, next to a little bakery set back from the ocean. The bakery was brightly lit inside, and wonderful smells came from it as we passed. Heron hurried past the bakery, and we stopped at a fence and gate. She took me through the gate to a bright red building.

"The loomhouse," she said and went inside.

I looked around. Cloth and yarn were everywhere. Fabrics of all sorts hung on the walls, and there were three big looms. One of them was run by electricity. I had never seen a power loom before. It was working, turning out a fine golden cloth faster than any person could have done.

At last I was in the world I knew. The cloth called to my eyes and hands, and I wanted to touch it, to start work, to show Heron what I could do.

A dark-haired girl stood by one of the looms. She was almost as tall as Heron, with her hair fixed the same way and wearing the same blue shift.

Heron called to her. "Aster, come here. This is Path, my new Hand."

"Welcome," she said. "I am Aster. A Hand also. But this is my last year."

"And I am Path." I looked up, met her eyes, and held them. She might be older, yes, and she might have been Heron's Hand for years, and she might have learned much. But I would show this girl the best I had and dare her to equal it. Finally she looked away.

Heron said, "Aster, show Path where she will sleep."

Aster took me to a tent made of a cloth that was the same bright red as the loomhouse. Inside I saw two of everything: two sleeping mats on the floor, two chests, two chairs. I realized we would both be living there. She gave me some bread and fish and fruit.

"I know you must be hungry and tired," she said. "Eat this and sleep." Then she left.

So this was it. My journey was over. This would be my home and I would share it with this tall girl. I looked at the food, surprised by my sudden hunger. I fell asleep as soon as I finished it.

2

Bird

"Mouse," said the cat. He lay on his side in the front window, large and tiger striped. His name was Walset. His eyes were shut and he seemed to be dozing. Cats often talk in their sleep, usually about food or other cats. Which is what they talk about when they're awake, too.

I am Bird Speaks and live with my ma, Cypress, and my sister, Crystal, in the bakery next to the Weavers' Yard on the Banks.

In the front room of the bakery, we were setting out loaves, cakes, pies, and rolls, all we had made that morning, for the people who would come in for the midday meal.

The radio was playing as it always did, giving us yet another of the Turning Songs for Midsummer Day, now just a month away.

> I will shut my eyes
> And a thousand eyes will open.

All right, I thought. *I know this song.* I knew it last week. I knew it last year. I looked around the room, at my ma and Crystal happily at work, and wished for another life.

I had lived through a circle of thirteen years. Born in Vulture year, I had lived through them all: Vulture, Wheat, Sun, Turtle, Lizard, Moon, Ant, Cat, Fish, Bear, Snake, Rabbit, and Spider. Now it was near the end of Vulture year, and in a month the year would turn to Wheat again on Midsummer Day. I wanted to be out. Out in the world, out in the ocean, out with my friends, most definitely not in the bakery.

I had spent the last year with the other boys my age at Children's House, where we had been given our tattoos and begun to be men. But now it seemed like my friends had come of age and I had come to a stop. Most of my friends were doing new things, the things you do in your second circle of years. Some were going on to be Hands at one trade or another, moving to new places. My friend Rope would be a Hand on a Ship in a few months. Now that was something interesting. But I was stuck in the bakery, where the loaves seemed heavy as logs as I filled the shelves. I knew how to bake bread, cakes, pastry, and everything else we made at the bakery. And I was good at it, too. *Why keep at this*, I wondered. I didn't want to think that baking would be my world for the rest of my life. So I tried to make the best of it while wanting another life at the same time.

When we had finished, it was time to clean up.

"Bird. Crystal. Don't sit now," said Ma. "You know work's not done."

Work's never done with you, I thought.

"We have to clean up while we can. Get out the old, scrub, clean. You too." And true to her words, she began to clean as she spoke, wiping flour dust off the counters with a damp cloth, motioning for Crystal and me to pitch in.

And she was right, of course. Flour, yeast, sugar, salt, sticky bits of honey that got left behind, all the stuff of baking goes everywhere in a bakery, and it will accumulate and make homes for all sorts of things if you don't keep clean. I knew that well by my fourteenth year. We got busy. I moved the bins and sacks of flour, the empty crocks and vats for mixing and proofing the dough, and started to clear off all the tables and shelves so that we could clean them.

"Look, Bird, look!" came my sister's voice, sounding as if she had seen something wonderful.

I went to her and saw. In the back of a shelf was a big wolf spider, watching us. She was almost as big as my hand. Ma came, too.

"Oh, Crystal, that's a big one." She looked at the spider, silently acknowledging it as a gift to us. "You two know what to do."

"I'll take her, Crystal." Anything to get outdoors. I got a small pot and quickly placed it on top of the spider so she couldn't run away, and then I slipped the end of a spatula under the pot, careful not to hurt the spider's legs. I lifted up the spatula, with spider and pot sitting on it, and went out into the yard. "Ma, I'll be right back after I take the spider."

Now a spider is a creature of real power, and this was one of the biggest I had ever seen. It is Spider who weaves the web of the universe and who sits in the center of that web, feet on the threads of all things. This spider was a gift to us, and our gift in return would be to help her on her way. I would treat her with respect. Respect demanded that if she happened to be someplace she didn't really belong, like on a bakery shelf, then it was up to me to put her on the path to the place where she did belong. And that place was across the fence.

Our bakery was next to the Weavers' Yard, and Spider was special to them. Spiders would always have an honored place there. Weavers would never disturb a spider or her web, and counted their presence a blessing. So I brought the pot to the fence separating us from the Weavers' Yard, lifted it off the spatula, and let the spider fall to the ground on the other side. She immediately ran into the yard and disappeared under a wooden table.

"The gift moves," I said, and Spider returned the gift immediately—I saw a girl hurrying with a bundle of deep red cloth in her arms. She wore a light blue tunic spattered with spots of dye. Her hair was brown, curly, and tied in a knot on top of her head, the way the weavers do. But it was her face that caught me. It was the face of someone with real purpose, real conviction. She was hurrying through the Weavers' Yard, and her eyes, her whole face, were focused and intent on what she was doing, on her work and her way in it. And where those eyes saw, her whole body followed, quickly, not a movement wasted, just graceful. I stood and watched her carry her cloth to a big wooden rack. Her movements were so precise and quick and there was so much delight in what she was doing that she seemed like a spirit and not a person, like a spirit that lives in a stream or in the woods, or in a cave and that spirit is part of the place, and embodies it. And you know that when you are lucky enough to see that spirit, you have seen to the center of the place, seen its reason for being. That is how she was to me in that moment. The spirit of the Weavers' Yard, spirit of the bright cloth.

She pulled the red cloth off her shoulder in a single strip, letting it fall length by length onto the rack without a fold or wrinkle, until it was all laid out before her, tight and flat. I was fascinated by her. By her quick delight. I wanted those eyes to see me. I wanted that gaze, that certainty, to focus on me, if only for a little while. I just wanted her to look at me, to see me, to acknowledge my presence across the fence.

She wouldn't look at me. At first I tried to catch her eye. But whenever it seemed she was about to turn my way, she'd go back to her work. I waved to her. Nothing. I jumped up and down, waving my arms over my head. She turned, holding a big piece of cloth in her hands. And just as her eyes were about to meet mine, she spread the cloth in front of her face, hiding behind it. I knew then that she had seen me, that she was playing with me. So I stood on my head in the sand by the fence and whistled loud and long, as hard as I could. I can whistle very loud. And that did it.

The girl stood still, looked at me face on with those bright eyes, looked a question, all of a sudden very serious. I stood up and faced her. No one had ever looked at me like that before. I felt she could look right through me and see inside me. And she must have liked what she saw because of what she did next. Without taking her eyes off me, she went to a long table with two pots on it. She put each arm into a different pot, almost up to the elbow. The pots were full of dye. She took her arms out of the dye and held them straight up over her head. One arm came out blue, blue as the sky around the moon, blue as the shallow sea after a storm. The other arm was red as blood. Slow drops of color ran down her arms, past her shoulders, into her shift, each one tracing a stream of color on her skin. Still she looked right at me. Then she took the first two fingers of each hand and drew a line of color across her forehead. The blue and red came together in a purple line that she traced down her cheeks to her throat. Purple like flowers. Purple like the first dawn sky. Then she put her arms down, smiled at me, and left, moving quickly. For the first time I noticed her tattoo, something green running around her leg to her foot.

I stood there for a long time, remembering how her skin had looked as it came blue and red from the dye, remembering her smile as she turned away. And that was how I first saw Path. Of course, I didn't even know her name then. But I made sure to find out as soon as I could.

3

Path

I knew what he wanted. Me. As soon as I saw him looking at me, as soon as I saw his hungry eyes, I knew he wanted me to look at him, to see him too. But I made him wait for it. Let him show me what he'd do, how far he'd go. And he put on a show, I'll give him that. Standing on his head and whistling, that was pretty good. But I could do better. So I put my arms in the dye and let the color take me. And it hurt. I didn't know it was going to do that, but I didn't care. I let that boy see all he wanted and never took my eyes off him while I did it. *You wanted to see me, baker boy, well, this is your time. Dare you to look away.* And he didn't, not once. I had him, and it felt good in a strange way. Felt like something was pushing me to show him more. Push me and I push back. In Boon I would jump from one branch to the next, one rock to the next, and dare my cousins to follow me. I would jump farther each time, not caring about the leap or the fall, until no one would follow me. And this was like that. I only thought I was going to show him the colors on my hands, not paint myself for his eyes. But I did. And all the time my skin itched more and more and began to hurt.

I turned away from him, holding my smile against the pain, and ran to the loomhouse. And there was Heron, right in my face, with Aster beside her looking at me in disbelief.

"Path. Look at you. What you have done."

"It hurts," I said.

"Yes," she said, "that it does." She punctuated every other word by hitting the ground with her staff. "It's a good thing you found me now."

Heron limped off ahead of me, quick as always. She led me out the back of the loomhouse, and to the freshwater tanks. She set water to boil.

"Watch and learn."

I didn't know what she was doing but knew better than to interrupt. She would tell me. She added white powder to the boiling stuff, stirred it, added cold water to cool it down, and poured it all into a bucket. Then she set the bucket in front of me.

"Put your arms in this, one at a time. Don't let it touch

your eyes or your nose or mouth. This is worse than the dye."

And it was. It burned like fire, but the dye started to fade. Heron took a cloth and rubbed some of the liquid over the line on my forehead.

"Hold still. You didn't blind yourself with the dye, so don't let this blind you either."

And then she was done. She looked me up and down.

"Well, now. You've got to get that stuff off you quick. Out of your clothes, into the ocean. Come on! Girl, you hurry up if you want to keep your skin."

So I did what I was told. I left my shift at her feet, ran to the beach, and jumped in. At the touch of the water the burning started to fade and I looked at my arms. The dye was almost gone, but my skin was pink and sore, as if it had been burned. I swam for a minute and came back for my clothes. Heron was still there, waiting for me.

"So," she said. "You are a lucky girl. And a hungry girl."

"Hungry?"

"Hungry for color, to wear it like that. So I will give you color. I will show you what you put your arms into. I had made that red and blue for your lesson today. But now we will start at the beginning."

She turned and headed for the loomhouse. "Aster!" she called. Aster followed us.

Inside the loomhouse it seemed dark after the bright sun. Heron quickly set several jars on a table. She put a mask over her nose and mouth and gave masks to Aster and me.

"Put this on, Path. We must not breathe what is in these jars."

She picked up one of them and opened it. Inside was a blue powder, dark as night. I bent over to see it more closely.

"Be careful. This must not get in your eyes. Even one grain would hurt you, as you should know. And you need to see, girl."

She opened another, which held a deep red powder.

"So. Red and blue, Path. Primary colors. We will mix them and make purple. But we will have to experiment to find the right purple. So we will make a solution of blue and a solution of red and mix them in different proportions to find the color we want. And then we will mix all the dye to that recipe."

She took a large ceramic pot and slowly poured the blue powder into it.

"Look. You make sure it all goes in without raising any dust that we might breathe or get in our eyes." Then she slowly and carefully stirred it with a spoon, looking for any lumps. Satisfied, she set the spoon down. "Now, watch what I do." She took a measure of water, about equal to dye, and slowly poured it into the pot, stirring all the time until the powder began to turn into a paste.

"This is what you want, Path. It must be an even, pasty consistency. Now. You take the red and do the same."

Aster handed me another big pot, and I took the jar with the red powder and slowly poured it into the pot.

"Be careful," said Heron. "Remember to keep it from getting into the air."

"We have masks," I said.

"Yes, but they won't filter all of it. So be slow, careful."

"Like this?" I said, going as slowly as I could.

"Like that."

And I was done. The red powder lay in the bottom of the white pot. I took a clean spoon and slowly stirred through it looking for lumps. As with the blue, there were none.

"That's it," said Heron. "Now the water."

"Here." Aster handed me a measure of water, and I slowly poured it into the powder, stirring just as Heron had, until it turned into a paste.

"Good, Path. Let me feel it." Heron took the spoon, stirred, and, satisfied, said, "Now. This is an acid dye. That means it will need other things. We will mix these pastes with more water to make our dye stock. But we will have to add more things to it for it to work. Here."

She showed us another jar, this one with a white powder in it.

"Sodium sulfide. It will slow down the dye so that it goes into the cloth evenly. And here." She took another jar but did not open it. "This is hydrochloric acid. After the cloth goes through the dye, the acid must be added to the dye bath to fix the color. And we must get it almost boiling hot. Aster, cover up the paste and we'll show Path the big dye pot."

We went outside to a big tank with a wooden platform all around it. Underneath was a big methane burner.

"This is where we dye the cloth."

We climbed up the steps to the platform.

"It all goes in here a batch at a time. First water, then dye, then cloth, then the sodium sulfide, then we heat it almost to boiling. Then the cloth comes out, the acid goes in, and we put the cloth back. And all the time we are doing this we stir it. When it is ready, we shut down the burner and let it cool. Then we take the cloth out and wash and dry it."

She leaned on her staff and looked at me. "Not how you did things with those old women in Boon, is it?"

"No, Heron, not at all."

The dyeing I had known was done in pots on a stove or in a fireplace or sometimes with no heat at all. And it was a slow process during which you would talk and joke as the fibers changed color. But this was different. I couldn't imagine how we could even lift that much wet cloth.

"But won't it be heavy? When it's wet, I mean, and hot, too."

"Yes, it will," said Heron. "Hot and heavy both."

Aster's eyes met mine. I would show this big girl I could lift anything she could, carry any load.

We went back to the loomhouse and set to mixing the

two dye pastes with enough water to make them liquid. We mixed them in big white enamel tubs with long paddles. The colors were so rich and the tubs so deep I thought I could get lost in them. When we were done, Heron gave us each a covered bowl.

"Now. Aster, take red, and Path, take blue. Here is a measure. Put one measure of dye stock into each bowl and follow me."

We did as we were told, and then she led us to a long wooden table at the edge of the yard. A row of clear glass jars stood on it, all empty. A pitcher of water was at the end of the table, and Heron poured a precise amount into each bowl.

"Now we are ready to mix them," she said.

And so we did. We mixed the red and blue in proportions ranging from ten parts red to one part blue all the way to one part red and ten parts blue. When we were done, we had a row of glass jars full of liquid whose color ran from deep red through magenta and purple and violet to dark blue. "Look, what do you see?" asked Heron. "There is a line of color changing before you, from fire to ocean. And where in that line shall our cloth be? Girls, you tell me. Use those eyes of yours."

Aster walked along the row of jars, looking at each one. *No, Aster,* I thought. *That's not how you do it. You need to see one thing, not many.* I walked several steps away from the jars until I could see the whole row at once, jewels in the sun.

And the answer was clear, obvious. Obvious to me but not to Aster, who was peering into the jars one at a time.

"Look," I said. "Look here." And I pointed to the jar three places from the middle on the red side. Aster looked up. She hadn't even got halfway down the row. Was she always this slow?

"This one, here." I touched the gleaming jar.

"And why?" asked Heron.

"Because the red is starting to shine through the blue. It has some fire in it. It shows where it is going. It calls you into it, into what it is going to do."

"The fire. Yes, girl, you are right." She studied me, silent for a while. Then she nodded as if I had passed her inspection. "I was right. You do know color, girl. Aster, you pay attention to her. She has things to show you."

Aster pulled herself up and looked hard at me. I gave it right back to her. We emptied the row of jars and poured the mixed dye into a jug. Later we would take it to Battery House and give it back to the trees, which, Heron said, would use anything.

"You come with me," Heron said and led me out into the yard. "I was right when I saw you. But I didn't know how far you would go."

She kept walking, eyes straight ahead, talking about me but not to me. I followed.

"It is not enough to be a good weaver. It is not enough to know and do. Aster has that. My other Hands had that. But what you have is different."

Then she turned around, pinned me with her gaze.

"You have the look," she said. "The look into things, the look that won't let go. That was me when I was young. I had it, too, like you do. You're hungry and eager and fast, and you love the color and the cloth and what it can say. You know it speaks, don't you?"

I nodded.

"That's why I picked you for a Hand. Five years to train you, and in five years you'll make cloth as good as any. Any!"

She paused and set her staff in a new place on the ground.

"The look you have, that I have. It took me far and it will take you far, if you will learn. So learn this."

With that she pulled her tunic up to her breasts and showed me her belly. And there was her tattoo. It showed Spider in the center of her web, her web the universe. "I am Spider for you now," said Heron. "So you listen." She touched Spider's abdomen just below her navel. "Spider sits at the center of everything that is. She weaves the stuff of our lives. The stuff of the past and future. What we have, what we hold, what we lose. This web"—she spread her hand across the web tattoo and then let it reach out to take in the yard, the buildings, the beach, the ocean, the sky—

"this web is the way that everything is connected." Her eyes flashed at mine. "Path, you pull this web and Spider will pull back. You don't know how or where. But she will. What you did today was a big pull, put that dye on you. You could have blinded yourself. And to take on the color that way, well, you are asking Spider for something, pulling on the web like that. You will get it."

I rubbed my arms and face, which still burned from the dye.

"It still hurts," I said.

Heron snorted. "It hurts? Yes, it hurts. I will tell you about hurt."

She held out her staff.

"I pulled the web once, asked for more cloth in two months than I had ever made in a year. I got the cloth. And I got this, too, later." With those words she handed me her staff. I was surprised how heavy it was, how hard to hold. Bouncing on her good leg, she said, "This is what the dye can give you, pull hard enough. Make your nerves forget how to move."

"The dye did that?" I asked.

"It gets in through your skin if you're not careful. And I was not."

"Why?"

"I wanted the cloth, girl, why else? And Spider gave it to me. This leg, too, and the staff. All that for pulling her web."

And then her eyes hardened, stared somewhere past me. "And I would pull it again just as hard. Just as hard. So would you, I think."

She took her staff back. "This was Spider's gift to me," she said. "There is a gift for you too, girl. Bear it when it comes." With those words she pulled her tunic back over the tattoo and started to walk to the loomhouse. But she had more to say over her shoulder.

"You remember what is important. I brought you here because you had the look that said you would pull on Spider's web, pull hard. Well, I'm not disappointed. What you did today? You became cloth to the dye! Cloth. Your own skin craving the color, all to show to that boy."

I blushed then, my own blood's color, and she saw.

"Yes. I saw the whole thing, saw what he did to get you to look. And you were looking all along, weren't you?"

I didn't answer.

"Of course you were," she said. "You went to him finally. And for his eyes you became cloth to the dye. What will you become for my eyes, eh? You remember what is important. For you, now, I am important. Not that boy. Let the cloth speak to him, not you. Now, while you are my Hand, your time is mine. Not his"—she looked over the fence toward the bakery—"not anyone's. Mine." She paused, then closed her eyes. "Go now."

And I went, Spider in my mind. *I have pulled your web. What will you give me in return?*

4

Bird

My head was in a still-warm oven, which I was cleaning, scraping out all the bits of dough and flour that would otherwise burn and smoke at the next baking. But my mind was in the Weavers' Yard. I couldn't stop thinking about her. I kept seeing her arms come blue and red from the dye, kept seeing the colors blend into purple as she drew her fingers across her forehead. Who was this girl who painted herself, gave herself to my eyes? How could I see her again? She had given me something extraordinary, and I would have to equal it, to give back. I had no idea. But something would come, I was sure. I finished cleaning the oven and pulled my head out.

Crystal knew I was someplace else. "Bird, what is on your mind?" she asked.

"When I took the spider back I saw something," I said, wiping the sweat off my forehead.

"Saw something," she repeated, and took a bread pan from the sink to dry.

"In the Weavers' Yard. There was a girl." And I told Crystal what I had seen.

"That's quite a thing for a weaver to do," she said. "Heron will not be happy, I think."

"Have you ever seen her before?" I asked, rinsing my rag and hanging it up to dry.

"I think once or twice. But she hasn't been there long."

"I wonder if I'll see her again. I want to."

"You know how the weavers are," she said. "Heron doesn't let them out much."

"I know. But still."

Just then Ma came in.

"All right," she said. "You two have done well here." She surveyed the room with satisfaction. "And you know where we go now."

I knew well where we would go, and I was looking forward to it. We would go to Battery House. Ma never did like electricity. She tolerated it but would rather not have it around. If I used an electric light to read at night, she would somehow know and make me turn it off. She must have been able to hear electrons flowing or maybe smell them.

I tried to be careful, to turn on a light only behind the closed door of my room, but somehow she always seemed to know. Still, I wished we had more light in the bakery.

"Ma," I said, "why don't we get some more batteries so we can have more light at night?"

"Think, Bird," she said. "Why do you want it to be light when it is dark?"

"So I can do things, Ma, things I want to do. I can read, explore in the night, see in the dark."

She threw up her hands. "See in the dark? That is what you will not do. You use your electricity to make light, and then you see in the light because you have made the dark go away. All the light in the world will not help you see in the dark."

Ma picked up a towel and started to wipe the counter, which was already clean. She turned and glared at me. "You are seeing in the light, and what you want is to carry light around with you. You want to see in the dark, then the first thing you do is turn off the lights. Then your hands will see, or your nose. Or your ears, like a bat."

"But Ma, I just want to read before I go to bed."

"I know you do. And you can use an oil lamp for that. Electric light is different. It goes too far, it's too white. It's like having your own little sun with you and so, before too long, you forget about the moon."

When she said that I knew what would come next. The old times.

"Bird, the people in the old times carried the sun with them all the time and everywhere. They believed in the light, believed they could walk in it all their lives. But whenever they carried the light, they carried the dark, too. Bottled up inside them. The more light they shone outside, the more dark inside. And then one day the dark took them."

This speech could go on. But this time she kept to the gist of it, that electricity was a mixed blessing at best and one that hid as much as it revealed. As always, I saved my favorite question for the end of her speech.

"But what about the radio?"

"Bird. That is different and you know it."

I did know that it was different, partly because of my father, who spoke on the radio all the time. He was the radio. But I pressed on.

"When we use the radio, we are hearing a voice from far off as if it were right here. And we use it all the time. How can that be so different from lighting up the dark? Where there was dark there is light; where there was silence there is a voice. It seems the same to me, Ma."

She threw down her towel and turned off the radio.

"Enough, Bird. You know the difference well enough. The radio is a thing that helps keep us all together. It is not solitary, it is not there to banish silence. It is not a boy with a light. It is a voice for all of us."

And she turned the radio back on again, playing yet another of the Turning Songs.

> Somewhere inside you is something so precious
> Pearl in the oyster, white as the moon
> And late at night when no one's watching
> You might take it out and let it light up the room.
> This is the thing you've got to get rid of,
> The thing you've got to lay down.

We closed up the bakery and set off for Battery House later that morning. We needed to have extra batteries for the baking we would do for Midsummer Day, and we had a load of used-up batteries to exchange for them. We piled them in the cart and set off.

Ordinarily we used little electricity at the bakery, and we had one battery tree of our own, which took care of our needs. But there were a few things that needed extra power, especially the warming ovens used for proofing dough. The warm moist air inside them was perfect for letting the dough rise before baking. The ovens would run nonstop in the week before Midsummer Day and would exhaust all the power we had in two or three days. The bakery's single battery tree would not be enough to keep them charged. So right now we needed more.

This time of year, Battery House was a busy place. Everybody needed more electricity, more batteries, more light.

I knew that Sparrow and Bright would be busy for the next week. It was not really a house, but more a large shed, closed at one end where Sparrow and Bright lived. Behind it were the trees themselves, acres of them.

When we got there, Bright was waiting. *Hoping to see Crystal*, I thought. She had a crush on him.

"Cypress, Crystal, Bird, it's that time of year again, huh?"

"Yes, it is," said Ma. Crystal pushed the cart full of old batteries to him.

"Here. These are for you."

He took the cart and wheeled it under the shed, sorting the old batteries by kind and tossing them in bins. Later he would crush, grind, and spread them around the trees. There was precious stuff in those batteries, and the trees would reuse all of it. Behind the shed were the trees themselves, long rows set in deep pits full of rocks and pebbles and ground-up old batteries and seawater. A few were small like the one we had at the bakery, but most were tall, taller than anything on the Banks except the radio tower.

Bright led us out of the shed and under the trees. It felt like walking into another world, suddenly dark and cool; the trees always turned their leaves to catch as much sunlight as they could. As far as they were concerned, light that reached the ground was light wasted.

Their leaves were long, almost like wings. And they were black, blacker than anything else, because they absorbed every sort of energy that touched them, from radio waves to infrared and x-rays. The leaves always felt cool to the touch, eager to absorb even the little heat they could get from your fingers. Whatever they took in they turned into electricity. Some of them stored it in batteries that grew on the trees like fruit; other trees transmitted the power through their own metal roots; and still others had lights on them that could light up a huge area at night, powered by a big battery in the trunk of the tree.

"So what for you this year?" he asked, leading us between the trees. "Maybe you would like a light tree. I have some small ones, small enough to fit right on your cart, and you could roll it home. Set the tree in the yard for a day, and it will store up enough energy to light the bakery all night for a week. It comes in its own pot, and all you have to do is give it seawater now and then. How about it?" He winked at Crystal, knowing Ma would never want such a thing.

"No, Bright, I don't think we need anything like that."

"But wouldn't it be nice to light up the whole kitchen when we're working at night?" asked Crystal, teasing Ma.

I teased, too. "Yes, Ma, Crystal's right. We could work better if we could see more. You know how hard it is to see the scales and measuring cups with those oil lamps."

"Yes, they're hard on the eyes, especially when you've been baking late into the night."

We knew Ma was not going to waver. "No. I think we have done well with what we have and will do so again this year. Anyway," she said, pointing to the fenced grove where the biggest trees were, "I'm sure Heron will take all you have."

And she would take a lot. In the weeks before Midsummer Day, Heron would have several big light trees brought to the Weavers' Yard, so she and her Hands could work through the night. The glare from across the fence would light up my room.

Ma changed the subject. "Bright, what is your favorite thing that we bake?"

He thought for a minute and then said, "You know, what I like best are your meringues."

"Crystal," said Ma, "did you bring some?"

And of course she had, knowing they were Bright's favorite and wanting him to like her. She took a bag out of her pouch and handed it to him.

"There. For you. The gift moves," she said, blushing a little.

"It moves. And I thank you," said Bright. "I have something for you." He reached into his pocket and pulled out a battery. "Every once in a while one of the trees will put out one of these."

He held the battery out for us to see. It was different. Usually the batteries are dark green or brown. But this one had a picture on one side, the face of a pretty woman. I had never seen one like it. Bright twisted the end of the battery, the way you do when you are installing it for the first time, and the picture began to move and speak.

> For all the times
> When you want to be sure,
> When you need to know the way,
> Biogreen makes the difference twenty-four hours a day.

While the woman said this, the picture changed to show her whole body, and you could see that she was carrying a baby on her hip and holding a light in one hand. She was standing in a forest, and the light showed the front of her house. She touched the door and gave the light to the baby, who gurgled with pleasure, and there was music and voices singing "Biogreen makes the difference twenty-four hours a day." Then the picture stopped moving, and the woman's face came back. Crystal took the battery from him.

"We see them like that every so often," said Bright. "When they made the DNA for these trees, they must have programmed messages into them, and many, if not all, of the batteries carried them, just like this one. After so many years of breeding the trees back and forth, the messages have been scrambled and lost, just random parts of the genetic code in there. But every once in a while you find one like this that works like it did long ago."

A face and voice from another world, I thought. *A world where the* lights shined twenty-four hours a day. Where there was no dark that you did not choose, where you could put out your hand and have anything at all.

I wondered what they were like, the people who had lived so long ago. Were they happy? The woman on the battery looked happy, with her smile and her baby and her house in the woods. And her light. But she was long gone, along with her baby and her home. What we had were the things her people had left behind.

They knew how to work with life the way Ma and Crystal and I work with flour and yeast and water. They made living things, like the battery trees, and the talking cats, and the buses, and the boats that grow from seeds, the Ships like the one where Rope will be a Hand, and more. And in a way, they even made us. Because they did things with humans, too, changed their very selves, so that we, their grandchildren many times over, are different. We live longer, we heal faster, we seldom get sick, and if we want to have a child, we have to think very hard to make ourselves fertile.

What happened to them? My father told me that there are two answers, and both of them are true. One answer you get if you read what they wrote about themselves when it happened. You'll read that all of the living things they made were unable to reproduce themselves. If you wanted a cat or bus or battery, you had to give something of value to the people who had the key to making more battery trees or talking cats or buses until, finally, those people had everything of value there was. You'll read that one day, someone took the key that let all these creatures reproduce and put it in a germ, a virus, and spread it all over the world. And when people found they could have as many battery trees and everything else they wanted, they fought a big war, and many people, more than half the world, died.

My father said that the other answer is the one you get if you ask anybody now. You'll hear that the whole world is dreamed by Bear in her den where she sleeps. And every so often, she turns over and wakes up a little, nuzzles her cubs, and starts to dream a new dream. For a long time she dreamed about a place where you could make things and lock them up and keep them forever. And then she started a different dream, and we are that dream right now, and it is the dream that matters.

I looked back down at the battery in my hand, saw the picture of the woman, still and silent. *Where are you*, I wondered. I thought of Bear dreaming in her den, and about Snake, who bites his own tail to make the circle of years. *Through the center of the circle*, I thought. *That's where.* I gave the battery back to Crystal as Bright led us to the shed. He filled our cart with batteries as we went, plucking them like fruit. Which they were.

When we stepped out from under the trees' cool dark into the light and heat, my eyes began to water from the glare. I blinked and looked around, and, across the shed, there she was. The weaver girl, with Heron's other Hand, a tall girl with a flower name. I had forgotten what it was. I looked at them, willing the weaver girl to look my way, to see me. But she wouldn't, just like before. I was sure she knew I was there. But she kept her back turned toward me. It would take more than standing on my head to get her to turn around, I knew. There was a way, and I would find it.

5

Path

It was still dark when Heron got us up. She came right into the tent with an electric light and turned it on.

"Up, up, you two. This will be a long day."

Before she was out the door, Aster was pulling on her shift and tying her hair.

"You better hurry," she said. "She means it. She means now. She always means now."

I blinked away sleep, then stood and pulled my shift over my head. By the time I had my hair tied, Aster was gone. I ran outside and saw her duck into the loomhouse.

Heron stood by the power loom, watching me as I came in.

"Today we begin to make room," she said, still looking at me. "We will weave and dye more cloth in the next month than you have made in your life. And most of it will be your purple, Path. But we start by making a place for it."

She went outside and opened the storage shed. It was full of wooden drying racks, stacked floor to ceiling.

"Aster," she said, "you show Path what to do, and be finished by midday." She went back to the looms, which stood empty, waiting for the warp to be wound and loaded.

"Come on," said Aster. She led me outside. "We have to set up all the racks in straight lines, over there." She pointed to the yard on the other side of the big dye vat. "We have to move all the stuff that's there now and put it up in the room where the racks are."

We got busy. There were all sorts of things to move—tables, water tanks, a wheeled cart with big doors and shelves on it. And then there were the racks themselves.

Aster went into the shed and picked up the first one. I followed right behind. Whatever she did, I would do, no matter if she was older and bigger. The rack felt as if it weighed as much as I did. Aster took her rack to the dye vat and set it up. I did the same and found the rack stiff with age, its hinges stuck. I pushed hard and finally it opened. I set it on the ground next to Aster's and went back for the next one. Back and forth we went all morning, finding ourselves in a slow rhythm between shed and yard. As the ground filled up with rows of drying racks, I began to realize how much cloth we were going to make. And all for the fire on Midsummer Day. When the last rack was set up, we put the rest of the things from the yard back in the storeroom.

Heron had been busy, too. We came back to the loom-house to see that she had wound the warp on the two manual looms and was busy with the power loom.

"So," she said. "You two are done. And in good time, too."

She stood, picked up a large cloth sack, and handed it to me.

"Here," she said. "You two fill this with the old batteries and take them to Battery House. And take that dye stock from yesterday, too. Exchange the batteries for fresh ones. And show this to Bright." She handed Aster a folded piece of paper. "Take some food with you. You can eat as you go."

She turned back to the loom she had been working on, dismissing us without a word. We walked back to our tent.

"No wasted time with her," said Aster. "Never do one thing if you can do two." She reached into the cupboard and took out bread, fruit, and cheese and put them all in a bag. "We'll need water, too," she said and picked up two plastic bottles. She gave me one. "Let's go then."

We gathered up all the old batteries we could find, put them in the sack, and turned out of the Weavers' Yard and into the street. I could tell Aster was waiting for me to speak, but I didn't want to. I reached into the food bag, took out bread and cheese, and began to chew. After a while she ate, too. Neither of us spoke a word all the way to Battery House. I could feel Aster's eyes on me the whole time.

When we got there, no one was around. We waited a few minutes, and then I heard voices and saw people coming out from the grove of trees. A woman and a man, a girl and a boy. And the boy was the boy from the bakery. I wouldn't look at him. *Let him wonder.*

After they left, Aster introduced me to Bright, and we exchanged batteries. She gave him Heron's paper, and his eyes widened when he saw it.

"Five light trees?" he said. "You can light up half the island with those. You are going to be busy, aren't you?"

Aster didn't reply.

"Well, it's no problem. Tell Heron we'll have the trees there tomorrow."

When we left, Aster turned away from the road and headed for the ocean. She stopped at the water's edge.

"I know you don't want to talk," she said. "I know you don't like me. But I don't care. If we're going to work together, we have to talk. We have to know each other."

I didn't know what to say. Aster began to walk through the shallow water.

"What you did yesterday, with the dye. That scared me. I need to trust you. I need to know you're not going to do something crazy like that with me."

I was angry now. I would never do anything to hurt the cloth. Or her. Who did she think I was?

"It was that boy, wasn't it?" she asked. "The one back there at Battery House. The boy from the bakery."

I nodded.

"I thought so," she said. "I know what you're doing. You're playing with him, and that's trouble. If you go further with him, Heron will get mad. And you don't want that."

"So?" I asked.

"So you *can* talk," said Aster, rolling her eyes. "And I'm right. When Heron's mad, life is awful for everybody, not just you. So."

She was making fun of me. I had to follow her, walking in the shallow water. The waves moved back and forth like a shuttle through the warp of our steps. If I had been sure of the way back, I'd have run.

"Enough of that," she said. "Where are you from?"

"I'm from Boon. In the mountains way to the west of here."

"What was it like? I mean, I've never been there."

She wanted my story. I would keep it short. "We raised sheep. My whole family did."

"Did you live on a farm, with barns and fields?"

"No, we lived with the sheep, mostly. We lived in tents and moved around with them."

"So you must feel right at home here. In a tent."

"No, this tent has a wooden floor. And it's much bigger and more solid than what we had. Everything we had was portable. We would pick up the tents, the sheep, the family, and move."

"That's so different from me. In Lanta we lived high up in a big building. It had ten floors, and we lived on the eighth. Just my father and mother and brother and me."

"You lived with both your parents?" I asked, curious in spite of myself.

"Yes," she said. "I know it's unusual, but it worked for us. What was your family like?"

"Like I said, it was big. The whole family had a name. The South Fork Family, because our sheep lived in pastures all along the South Fork of the New River near Boon. There was my father, Ram, and all the aunts and uncles and cousins. There were seventy-five of us, I think."

Aster looked at me in surprise. "That's a lot. And you think there were seventy-five? You don't know for sure?"

"They would come and go sometimes. And we weren't all together. Different groups would go to different pastures with the sheep. There were two thousand sheep. And when I started to learn to weave, I came off the mountain and lived with the weavers by the river. So I was away from the sheep for a while before I came here."

"What about your mother?" Aster asked.

I waited. I didn't want to say anything about my mother. Not now. Not tomorrow. The Sun and Moon bounced against my chest with each step. I watched little gray birds run in and out of the water, sticking their beaks into the wet sand to find things to eat. When we came near, they flew away.

But the silence just hung there. I could tell that Aster would wait me out. So I told a little. "She was a dancer. From Rollydee."

"What was her name?"

"Cat Sign."

"And how did she get to Boon? With two thousand sheep." Aster laughed.

"I don't think it's funny," I said. Why did this girl keep at it?

"I'm sorry," she said. "It just seemed like such a different life for her."

It *sure was*, I thought. "She came into the mountains to teach people to dance. She thought she'd go back to Rollydee after a little while, but she met my father and stayed. What about your parents?"

"They are Falls Far, my father, and Smooth Rock, my mother. He works with the city water supply, and my mother is a weaver. She taught me to weave and got Heron to take me as a Hand. I knew about Heron from when I was little. And I thought that what she made was the most beautiful stuff I had ever seen. I thought that if I could ever learn to do even a little bit of what she did, I would be happy forever. And now here I am with her, a Hand. I've got one more year to go, and then I can go back to Lanta and make cloth with my mother."

She would work with her mother. I remembered my mother dancing, remembered her carrying me over her head as if I could fly. Lucky Aster. I touched the Sun and Moon pendant, and Aster saw me.

"What's that?" she asked.

"Nothing. Just an old thing." *You can have my words. But not this.*

"Can I see?"

"No, it's nothing." Would she not let go? I was silent, determined to wait her out this time. She looked at me hard all at once.

"Okay. That's something special, then. Too special to talk about."

"Yes," I said. "It's for me to know. Not you." I was angry at this girl for pushing me. I would find my time to push back.

"I respect that," she said. "So tell me about your work. Did you learn to weave in Boon? Heron talked about you before you came. She said you were very good."

"Yes. I apprenticed with two weavers in Boon for Spider and Vulture years."

"Then they must have taught you a lot."

"So what is it like here?" I asked, thinking to change the subject and get Aster to talk about herself again.

"It's pretty quiet," she said, "except when there are storms. At least one a year will be bad enough to put water in the loomhouse."

"What do you do?"

"We take the looms out when we have time, and if we don't, we get them up off the floor and pray Spider doesn't pull them down."

"It sounds frightening."

"It is frightening. I was here when the sea took whole groups of buildings. And some people, too, who wouldn't leave."

"Why did they stay?"

"I guess because they like it. They like being someplace where things are uncertain, where the land moves a little every year."

She paused, watched the ocean for a while. I was glad for the quiet.

"It's lonely here," she said.

"I like being alone."

"At first I tried to have friends, but Heron let me know not to."

"Why?"

"Because she wants our *work* to be known. Not us. She wants people to see us walking down the road and remember what we have done, and to remember her especially. For the work, the cloth. That's the first thing I found out here. The cloth is everything. And the cloth is her."

I remembered Heron showing me the ocean yesterday, her first lesson to me. "And how about you? If the cloth is everything, what are you?"

"Hands and feet and hard work, that's what I am. But it's almost over. This is my last year, and then I can have my life back and have all the things I learned, too."

"This is my life," I said. "It's what I know. Color, pattern, beauty."

"It's not enough."

"For me it will be," I said. "I can make it be anything I want. And I will make it be enough."

"You're just like her," Aster said.

"Who?"

"Heron. That's exactly what she would say. No wonder she likes you so much."

We walked the rest of the way in silence.

6

Bird

The bakery was hot, and the light breeze coming through the windows gave little relief from the heat of the ovens. But I could deal with this. I knew how to be somewhere else in my mind. I had known how to do this for as long as I could remember. My hands would work, busy at whatever task Ma had given me, but my mind would be far away. This helped make working in the bakery a little more bearable, and I enjoyed the time I could spend in my imagination. Like now.

All the way home from Battery House, I hadn't been able to get the moving picture of the woman and her baby out of my head. When I closed my eyes, I could see them on the side of the battery. I wondered about them.

Back at the bakery, we went to work. As my hands found flour and pans and set them in their familiar places, my mind found the woman and her baby. Snake bit his tail and I looked through the circle. There they were, standing by the door of their bright house in the woods. It was so clear, so real in my imagination, that I knew I could reach out, open the front door, and go in. And so, as I opened the spice cupboard to return a jar of coriander, that's what I did.

The lights were bright inside the house, and there were soft things all around. And lots of metal and glass and plastic. There was stuff everywhere: pictures, books, enough chairs and soft couches to seat fifteen people just in one room. And I could see more chairs and a table through a doorway in front of me. Under my feet the floor was springy. When I looked down I saw a carpet as fine as grass and almost as deep. Electric motors hummed around me, doing what, I did not know. I walked through the room past the stacks of books and a large video screen on one wall. I went into the next room where the table was, and all the lights came on. So this is where they ate. Eight chairs surrounded the shiny wooden table, and in the next room there was a stove, cooler, and counters for preparing food. There was food in the cooler, enough to feed Ma and Crystal and me for weeks. There were dishes and pots and pans and containers, enough for a town. And it was all brand-new.

These people had kept everything they ever had. Once they got a thing, they never let go of it, so that even though they already had one pot to cook in, they would get another and keep the first one, and then *another after that, and keep them all. There was no empty place here, no room for becoming, no room for the gift. It was full.*

I was so absorbed in all this that I had stopped working. Ma saw.

"Bird, where are you? Not here, not in the bakery."

I came back to myself, the woman and baby and their house in the woods gone from my mind.

"I'm sorry, Ma. I was just thinking."

"Thinking. And where did your thoughts take you that was more important than here and now?"

"I was thinking about the pictures on the battery Bright gave to Crystal, that's all."

"Hmm. Better you think about what is in front of you."

What was in front of me was the countertop, covered with a layer of flour and stacks of baking pans. I went back to work, telling myself to be more careful and not let my mind wander so far. Not right now, anyway, when there was so much to do and Ma was watching.

Still I kept thinking about the house in the forest and all the things it was stuffed with. Could they have really lived like that in the Old Time? What would you do with all that stuff? What would you do when you ran out of room? What if there were other rooms in the house just for holding more stuff? Maybe there were rooms full of shelves and racks. Maybe there was one room filled entirely with cups, floor to ceiling. And another with shirts, all of them new, all of them different. *Why not?* I thought. These people wore clothes all the time. You almost never saw a picture of them in their own skin. I laughed.

Crystal heard. "What's so funny?"

"Oh, nothing. I was trying to imagine what life was like for the woman and baby on the battery that Bright gave you."

"You think too much, Bird. You are your father's child," she said and turned back to the sink full of oven racks she was washing.

"And whose child are you, then?"

"No child. I am my own woman. Like Cat. Old enough to do what I want."

"Bet you'd like to be Bright's woman," I said.

She threw soapy water at me, laughing and blushing at the same time.

We were getting ready to bake far more than we could use, far more than the town could use. Everybody would do this for Midsummer Day. Some people, like the weavers next door, made things all year for that day. Of course, we couldn't do that. Food had to be fresh, ready to eat and the best you could make, even if you knew no one would eat it.

It would be a large amount of stuff, but it was not like

the room of cups or the room of shirts I had imagined. We would take it to the Circle at Midsummer Day, eat it, give it up, and use it, and what was left we would burn at the end of the day. All of it. And then we would go home to the empty place, a place the next year would fill. Without the empty place, there would be no gift the next year, no turn of the wheel, no step on the way.

Life in the house in the woods must have been like holding your breath all the time, and holding more of it every day. I wondered where it went, what happened when you put the last shirt in the room of shirts and then tried to put in one more, the one that wouldn't fit. Did the whole house burst then? Probably not. Probably they just built another room. Why not? They had everything else.

After the evening meal, I sat in my room thinking about the weaver girl. She wouldn't look at me at Battery House that afternoon. But I was sure she had seen me and knew who I was. And I wanted to see her again, wanted to talk to her. I wondered what her voice sounded like. But if she wouldn't look at me, what could I do to get her to notice me? I decided to ask Crystal.

I went across the hall to her room and knocked.

"Come in," she said. She was lying on her back on her mat, looking at the battery Bright had given her.

"So you like it, too," I said.

"Yes, it's different. Do you think she's pretty?" She handed me the battery with the smiling woman on the side.

"She has too much paint. Her skin is too white and her lips are too red."

"Paint?" asked Crystal. "What about your weaver girl? Now there's some paint."

"I wanted to ask you about her."

"Oh, really?" In a moment she was sitting up on her mat, all attention. "Ask, then," she said.

"When we were at Battery House today, and she was there, she wouldn't look at me. I tried to get her to notice me, but she wouldn't. So what can I do? I can't stand by the fence all the time and hope she shows up. Ma will get mad."

"Heron, too," said Crystal. "Bird. If she won't look at you, give her something to look at. Something you made. A gift. Leave it someplace where she'll find it and know it's from you."

"And then?"

"And then it's her choice. If she takes up the gift, she will return the gift. And then you'll know."

"But what can I make?"

"What can you make? Of all the people I know, Bird, you are the last one to have to ask that question. You will think of something. You always think of something."

"Then I will think," I said. "Thanks, Crystal."

"For you, anytime."

I went back to my room and wondered what to do. I

had a collection of special objects—bones, rocks, feathers, things that had struck my eye. I spread them out on the floor and wondered if this was my room full of shirts. I picked up a fish's head, the bone cool and white, and held it up. In a minute I knew what to do. I took clay and feathers and set to work, making a birdman. *A little like me*, I thought, gluing feather to bone. What words would this bird speak to the weaver girl? Words that she would hear, words she would give back, I hoped. I took the clay body and set it in a slow oven overnight to harden. The next morning I got up early, retrieved it, and fitted the fish skull and feathers back on the now-hard body. I liked it.

But where could I leave it so she would find it and know it was from me? The only place I could think of was by the fence where I had released the spider and seen her for the first time. So that's where I went. I stood there for a long time and remembered how her skin looked as it came blue and red from the dye. And her smile as she turned away. Finally I took my birdman and left it on the ground on the weavers' side of the fence, standing on its head as I had done. "Please find it," I said as I walked away.

7

Path

I had never been so busy in my life. I had spent long days with Bone and Blue Leaf, especially in the summer, weaving warm things for the coming cold. But with Heron it was different. We would use the power loom to weave thousands of square feet of cloth, all for Midsummer Day, and then we would dye it. But first the weaving.

Heron called us to the loomhouse at first light.

"Path, you listen. Aster has been over this ground before, but for you it will be new. So."

She stood by the power loom.

"While you two were gone to Battery House, I was busy." She laid her hand on the warp beam of the power loom. She had wound it with a warp eight feet wide, all bleached linen. "Now it's your turn. You girls tie this up. We will be weaving by midmorning." Heron looked at us, daring us to ask a question. We didn't speak. Satisfied, she nodded and left.

"Start in the center and work out," said Aster.

"I'll take the left side," I replied.

You may think that weaving is a simple process of moving the shuttle through the separated strands of the warp, back and forth, back and forth, pulling the beater after each pass to keep the weave tight and even. You watch the cloth appear in front of you, one thread's width with each pass of the shuttle through the shed, and you would be right as far as you go. But that is the quick part of weaving. Getting the loom ready to weave often takes more time than the weaving, because you have to get the strands of the warp to pass through all the parts of the loom and tie them to the beam in order to have something for the shuttle to pass through.

Heron had calculated the necessary length of the warp and the number of individual strands in it, and wound it all on the warp beam. It was our job to take it the rest of the way. As always, the warp from the last piece woven on the loom was still in it, saving us having to thread each individual strand through heddle and reed. All we had to do was tie the ends of the new warp to the old, pull the new warp through, then tie it to the cloth beam, and we would be ready to weave. Simple. Except that we were preparing to weave a cloth that was eight feet wide with thirty warp ends per inch. That's almost three thousand strands in the warp—three thousand knots to tie, each one strong and tight and small enough to pass through the dents of the reed without coming loose or breaking. Our hands would be cramped and sore long before we were done.

The power loom filled one end of the loomhouse, all light wood and metal. It was almost fifteen feet wide, and there was enough room inside for both Aster and me between warp beam and upright. And there we sat, each on a stool. We began to tie up, working quickly in silence. My fingers made square knot after square knot, each like the one before it, joining one strand to another with a double loop and twist, feeling the tension in the warp as I pulled the knot tight. After a hundred knots, I was lost in the rhythm of it. Then Aster spoke.

"This is what I do well," she said, fingers moving, tying one knot after another as she spoke. "My hands are what I have. They are quick and precise, and they don't make mistakes."

"So?" I said. What was she talking about? Of course she had good hands. So did I, and neither one of us would be there if we didn't.

"You have good hands, too," she said. "Heron talked to me a lot about that before you came."

Now I was interested in spite of myself. "What did she say?" I asked.

"She said she had finally found the girl who had the hands and the eyes both. That was what she said."

Me, I thought. "She talked about my eyes?"

"Yes," said Aster. "She talked about your eyes, especially when we would mix dye. Heron sees so well, and she has been looking for someone who can see as well as she can."

"And that's me?"

"That's you."

As we talked and tied, we moved away from each other, a thirtieth of an inch with each knot. Every so often one of us would move her stool toward the back to gain work room.

"But there are some things Heron doesn't see at all," said Aster.

"How do you mean?"

"I mean this. Heron has spent years and years, maybe her whole life, looking for someone. A young girl who is like the young girl she used to be. And now she's found her. So what is she going to do with her?"

"She's going to teach me the cloth, teach me what she knows," I said.

"And what will you give back in return?"

"I'll give her the best I can do. My work, my best work."

"No. She wants you to give her own self back to her. She

looks at you and sees a mirror. Sees herself as a girl. The girl she wishes she had been."

"Why?"

"She is a sad and unhappy person, and she thinks that having someone like you to teach and bring up in the cloth will make her happy, but it won't."

"How do you know this?" I asked, moving my stool back another foot.

"How do you think?" she asked. "She tried it with me. For the first two years I was here, that was what she did. And I always disappointed her. But she kept trying, kept expecting me to see what I could not see, kept expecting my mind to keep up with hers."

"What happened?"

"It was awful. I went to bed every night knowing I was not good enough, and knowing that the next day would bring me another chance to fail her. And that's how it was until she gave up on me."

"She gave up?"

"One day we were weaving, and she expected me to know the treadling of a piece just from looking at a sample of the cloth. And I could have figured it out if I had enough time. But that's not what Heron wanted from me. She wanted me to look and know, all at once, the way she does. The way you do. And she looked at me, at the cloth in my hands, and said, 'All right.' She wrote out the treadling for me and after that stopped trying to make me be other than I am."

"And things were better then?" I asked.

"Yes. She started to notice what I could do. And production began to go up. She paid attention to my hands and stopped wishing for my eyes."

Aster flexed her hands. "Then she started looking for you."

"For me?"

"Yes. You must understand this about her. She doesn't give up."

"But you said she gave up on you."

"She gave up on me, yes. But she didn't give up on finding someone with the eyes and hands, someone like her."

"And she found me."

"She found you. What she doesn't see, for all her vision, is that now that she has found someone as good as she is, she has met her match. Path, she is going to be very hard on you."

"Hard on me?" I asked. "What can she do? She wants me to weave, I will weave. She wants cloth, I will give her cloth. I think she will be happy with that."

Aster stopped tying and looked at me.

"It's not the cloth, Path, it's Heron. She will look at you and see herself, her young self, and want to make things right for that little girl. She is not going to see you."

I wondered about Heron as a little girl. I couldn't imagine it, couldn't see her any other way than tall, lame, gray-haired. So I asked, "What does she want to make right?"

"It's something about her mother."

Her mother. I stopped tying my knots and held the Sun and Moon tight in my hand. "What about her mother?" I asked.

"She was a weaver and dyer, like Heron," Aster said. "But Heron was never good enough for her."

"How do you know this?"

"From little things Heron told me, things she let slip. I keep my ears open. Over four years she's told me more than she knows, a little at a time."

"And you think she wants me to be the child, she the mother? Is that it?" I let go of the Sun and Moon. "I will give her my work, what I do. I will give her the cloth. That's what her mother wanted from her, wasn't it?"

Aster shook her head and went back to tying, knot after knot. We worked that way for a while, slowly moving away from each other to the edge of the warp. I thought she was talked out. But no.

"Path," she said.

"What now?"

"When you put your arms in the dye the other day."

"What of it?" I asked, wondering if that one act was going to follow me the whole time I was there.

"Heron talked to you after, didn't she?"

"Yes."

"What did she say?"

I thought about not answering but knew Aster wasn't going to let go. So I told the truth.

"She said I was pulling the web. She showed me her tattoo."

"Spider."

"Yes. She said she had pulled the web and got her lame leg for it. Said she had got cloth, too, more in two months than she had made in a year."

"And she liked that in you, too, didn't she?"

I remembered what Heron had said about how she would pull the web again, about how I would, too. But I didn't tell Aster that. "What did she like in me?" I asked.

"The part of you that pulled the web, that's what she liked. She will push you. Where she believes you are like her, she will push you."

I didn't reply but kept on tying my knots. By now there were fewer than two hundred to go. But Aster wouldn't give up.

"You will have a choice. To please her or disappoint her. I disappointed her for years, and that was bad. But you are going to please her, and that will be worse."

Finally I'd had enough. "I can take care of myself, you know," I said. I put down the warp and stood up, for once looking down on Aster. "I had to learn that to get by. I was always the smallest and the lightest. But I made sure I was the best. At everything. No one could hurt me then. No one could surprise me, because I always got there first. And I will do that here. I will show Heron. And you." I was angry, breathing hard, my voice shaking. Aster looked up at me standing over her and did not blink.

"Yes," she said. "As I told you. You're just like Heron."

"I am not," I said and waited for Aster's reply. But she was silent. Talked out at last.

We finished tying up the loom in silence, and then it was time to pull the warp through the loom. I always loved this part of weaving, because I was pulling the old warp to get the new one through the heddles and reed, and it felt like I was pulling on every warp that would ever pass through the loom. The resistance and release in my fingers as the knots passed through the reed felt like the beginning of something wonderful. And not even Aster's words could take that away.

But I couldn't forget what she had said. If Heron wanted to push me, what could I do? I would push back, push with the cloth, with my hands and feet and everything else I had.

Heron returned as we were tying the last of the warp onto the cloth beam.

"And you are finished," she said. "Good. You go rest your hands. You think you are sore now, Path, wait until tonight. You will find out what it feels like to be a real weaver."

"I am a real weaver."

"Hah," she said. "When you are a real weaver the work comes to live in your body, changes you, makes you hurt in the night, stiff in the morning when you wake. Then you are a real weaver."

She pounded the floor with her staff to remind me how the work came to live in her. Then she picked up a shuttle, loaded a bobbin into it, and set the loom working.

I watched the shuttle fly back and forth, saw the cloth begin to emerge and wind around the cloth beam, the first of countless yards of white linen we would fold and carry and dye, all for Midsummer Day. I massaged my sore hands and left the loomhouse, walking through the yard. I added up in my mind what I had seen on the three days I had been there. Heron. The ocean. Aster, who would not leave me alone. And the boy from the bakery. For him I had dyed myself. Which took me back to Heron and pulling the web. And from there I remembered Aster's words.

I went to the fence where I had seen the baker boy. I wondered where he was, what he was doing, whether his work was as hard as mine. And then I saw something in the sand, a figure standing on its head just as the baker boy had done. I picked it up and looked at it.

It was a little clay person, with feathers for wings and a fish's skull for a head. It was funny, and I laughed. My first laugh in a long time.

I turned it over in my hands, felt how the clay and bone joined smoothly together, as if they belonged that way. *Really, it's good*, I thought. The baker boy had made it. I was sure. And I would give it back to him.

I took it to the dye tent where we keep the paints and inks and pens and brushes for writing on the cloth.

I painted the clay figure all red and blue and purple. I traced its features in black and gave it golden wings and a golden head and beak that might be laughing or about to bite, who knew? And I let it dry overnight and took it back early the next morning to the place where I had found it. I knew he would come for it.

8

Bird

All that evening I thought about her. I didn't want to eat, didn't pay attention to the dough set to rise for the morning baking.

"Bird, where are you?" asked my mother. "Not here, that's for sure. If you don't punch that down, we'll have no bread worth eating in the morning. And that's our busiest time."

So I turned to the dough and did as I was told.

I hardly slept at all that night, and as soon as I could the next morning I left the bakery and went back to the fence by the Weavers' Yard where I had seen the girl. Where I had left the birdman. I saw it from way off, right where I'd left it, and my heart sank. *She doesn't want it,* I thought. *It's not any good. Not interesting.* But when I bent to pick it up, I saw that she had found it. She had taken it, colored it, painted it, and made it into a thing of wonder.

The body that had been brown clay the day before was deep blue and red and purple, and the head and beak were gold, and the wings, too. Somehow she had given it an expression, so that the beak seemed to be smiling but dangerous, too. I marveled. Marveled at what she had done, marveled that she had done it for me. She'd talk to me now, I was sure.

Ma was waiting for me when I came back to the bakery. Hands deep in flour, she spoke. "And where did you get that?"

"I made it, but it was painted by the new girl over at the Weavers', Ma." I didn't want her to know I'd been paying so much attention to life across the fence. But she knew.

"So. You've looked for that girl, I know. And you've found her. Given her a gift and she's given it back to you. And now there will be something to give next. The back-and-forth will start. You're not ready for that. And Bird, she's a Hand. She's from someplace else, someplace far away. She'll be here for five years and then go back where she came from, wherever that was."

She gave me a look that said wherever that was, it was no place good; else why would she be there?

"But look what she did." I held out the birdman for her

to see more closely, and I could tell she was impressed in spite of herself.

"Well. It is well done. But Bird. That kind of person, a Hand from who knows where, she isn't the kind of person you need to spend your time with. Besides, old Heron will work her hard, hard. She won't have much time for anything but the cloth."

I thought again of how quickly the weaver girl was always moving, how she was always ready for the next thing even before the first thing got finished. And though I'd never seen Heron hit anyone with her staff, I'd seen her raise it in silent threat when things weren't done to suit her. I thought a minute and decided to press on with my mother. She seemed happy now, and the morning had gone well. With her, it was best to take the chance when you had it.

"I wonder where she comes from. Maybe someplace interesting. Maybe a city. Or an island somewhere."

"There's no telling, Bird. Heron travels far with her cloth, and her cloth travels farther still. People from all over have it. She's well known, you know, and for some people it would be a catch to have their daughter picked by her for a Hand." Then she laughed.

I kept on. "Maybe she would teach me how to paint like this. Teach me how to mix colors."

But this was as much as my mother would hear. She

stopped mixing flour and yeast and gave me her full attention.

"Bird. You are a baker. You have plenty to learn, and it is not about color. It is about baking, and flour and yeast and water and the heat of the oven, about hungry bellies and what to give them. Our bellies, too. You want to learn? There is more to learn in our craft than I can teach you, more than I or you can ever know. That is enough for you. Enough for anyone. In fact"—and here she added water to what she had mixed and pointed to the trough of wet stuff that would turn into fifty-two loaves in another couple of hours—"here is more than enough for you, right now."

I knew what to do. I took up the paddle and mixed the flour and yeast and water, added some honey and grated orange peel. This makes a bread that people like to have during the day, for the midday meal or else just to munch on whenever they want. It is kind of sweet and thick and it fills you up.

As the goo turned into dough, I had to push harder with the paddle and thought and thought about the girl. Where was she from, really? And what was her life like? Of course, she had just got here. She'd never been on the streets with the other kids, never been to the Circle for games or to learn any of the songs for Midsummer Day or even for just walking around. Maybe my mother was right. Heron would work her and work her, and that would be it.

Now the dough was dough, sure enough. So I rolled it into a big crock to rise for a while. I looked again at the birdman and wondered, What now? What could I do that she would notice? Because I knew she wanted me to. Wouldn't have taken the time to paint the figure if she weren't expecting something from me.

My hands and arms, covered with flour and honey and bits of the dough, made me think of the girl and the dye running down her arms, and then I knew what I would make for her. My own work, what I knew how to do. I would make her something to eat. Something special.

If Heron was famous in this part of the world for her cloth, well, we were famous in this town for sweet things. Or Ma was. Cakes, pastries, little pies that took only one bite, sweet biscuits you could carry all day and still they would snap when you bit them. People came to us for these things, and if they had to walk the length of the island, they were glad to go the distance. Because what we made was so good. And some things I could make even better than my mother. So I thought about what to make for the girl. It would have to be something best eaten cool and not fresh out of the oven, because I didn't know when I would see her. I couldn't plan to have something hot and ready and bring it to her. Which left a lot out. But there were the little pies. The one-cherry pie, for instance. We took the fresh cherries and soaked them in brandy for an hour, then rolled each in powdered sugar, wrapped it in a special pastry, and baked or fried it. I thought maybe the fried ones would be best because they are a bit crunchier on the outside and a bit juicier on the inside, since they cook so fast.

So that is what I did. Between punching down the fifty-two loaves' worth of dough my mother had left me and carding it into pieces and slipping it into pans to bake, I put together what I would need for a dozen of the little pies. Flour, shortening, cherries, and the brandy and sugar. The fryer was always hot. After the loaves went in, I set to make the dozen pies for the girl and put them in the hot fat as soon as the loaves came out. Within minutes they were cooling on the rack. They would be my return of the gift of the painted birdman. And in return, she would tell me her name.

I realized I would have to come up with an explanation for my mother. I was lucky she hadn't come back into the bakery from the front room and seen what I was doing. But I knew what to tell her. I wrapped the pies in a cloth and put them in a bag.

"Ma, I'm going to the Circle to see how they're doing." This close to Midsummer Day, the Circle would be full of people building stands and stalls for the feast, assembling the wood for the big fire. A town of a thousand people needed a big fire for Midsummer Day.

"I'm taking something to eat, Ma. The loaves just came out and I set them to cool." Then I showed her the little bag of pies. It's always best to let out a little truth so you can hide something else. I knew she wouldn't be happy with me making off with that many pies, but if she scolded me about that, maybe she wouldn't be wondering about what I was really doing.

"Bird, those pies. That's a lot, you know. You plan to eat them all?"

"No, Ma. You know how people like them. I'm going to give them away." All this was true, in a way. I was going to give the pies away, and I might go to the Circle, sometime. "Then when people want more, they'll know where to find them."

"Well, they will want more," she said. *Secretly proud*, I thought. "And you make them as well as I do."

Better, I thought.

"You go now. But be back before the rush time this evening. People get hungry. We'll all need to be here."

And I left. Out the front of the bakery, into the street, and left down the little hill that goes to the ocean. Then I sneaked around the back of the bakery, hoping Ma was still in the front room and unable to see me, and crossed over to the fence by the Weavers' Yard.

They looked busy. Strips of bright purple cloth were hanging in the sun, stretched over wooden frames. *Must be drying*, I thought. I wondered if it was the same dye I had watched run down the weaver girl's arms, watched turn to purple as the red and blue came together on her face. I looked for her, tried to see her quick step and tied-up knot of hair in the yard. But no sign of her. Then I saw her, coming out of the big tent in the middle of the yard. She disappeared behind some vats and came out with her arms full of long poles, for what I didn't know. Then she walked in my direction, and I knew she saw me. She put the poles down and came to the fence. I was surprised to see that her skin was almost its normal color again. How did she get the dye off? I looked at the tattoo on her leg. I could see that it was a line of bright green footprints and wondered where they went.

She stood in front of me, looked straight at me. I waited for a while, played the who's-going-to-speak-first game, and then thought to show her what I had brought. I took out one of the little pies, bit it in half, chewed the sweet stuff, and let her see the red insides of the half in my hand. It was as red as the cloth that covered the weavers' tents. I held it out to her, and she took it and ate it. I could tell she was surprised at how good it was. Most people are. And then they want more. I knew she did. Heron probably fed her oatmeal and dried fish. So I held out another and spoke my first words to her.

"This for you, in return for your gift."

She looked the question.

"Your name," I answered.

And then I heard her voice for the first time, soft and very low for a girl, speaking her name.

"Path Down the Mountain," she said. "The gift moves."

"It moves," I replied.

9

Path

I couldn't believe I told him my name. My name! And for a pie, of all things. I must have been hungrier than I knew, and hungry for what? Bad enough I ate the other half of the pie he had eaten, that his teeth had split. Hungry for him, too? After I spoke my name, he handed me another little pie. Then he told me his name.

"And I am Bird Speaks. But call me Bird. The gift moves."

"It moves."

He handed me a sack with more of the little pies in it and was gone. Baker boy. Bird.

I was left with his gift, left to consider what I had given him. I had not spoken my full name since leaving Boon, since the day I last walked the path that is my name. And it seemed forever ago, not just a week.

I sat down in the shade of the drying rack where I hoped Heron couldn't see me. I knew that I was doing what she had forbidden, but I would take the chance. I ate another pie and then another. They were good, really. And to think they made them at the bakery. I looked out over the fence then, but there was no sign of Bird or anyone else there.

I would have to go there sometime, I knew. The gift required it. And Bird, he was sly with his gifts. When you meet someone on the street and are introduced by a third person, it is very different from two people sharing names the way Bird and I did. It is a passing of the gift between two people. You receive, you give back, and that is the balance in the web, what keeps it tight. So I could blame myself. I gave him the sight of me with the dye. Gave more than I meant, too. And he gave me his birdman, and I painted it and gave it back. Then he gave me half a pie and tricked my name out of me with another one. And now I had a whole bag of pies, did have but I'd eaten most of them. I was at a disadvantage in the return of gifts here, and I didn't like it. I didn't like him knowing my name. When you give your name in return for a gift, you have given a great deal. I didn't want to be obligated to return gifts to him. But I could be sly with gifts, too.

I got up and thought of what to do.

I walked down the rows of drying racks, checking to make sure the cloth was tight and smooth, that no bugs or birds were getting on it, seeing that it was drying evenly. The sunlight would help set the dye in the cloth, both because of the warmth and because of the speed with which it dried. So we had to lay out the pieces whole and let them dry at once.

Heron knew that it was a good show for people passing by. It was a gift for the eyes, and in that a kind of challenge, saying to all comers: "Have you ever seen purple as purple as this?" And of course the answer was no. There is no purple as purple as this. By laying it all out in plain view like that, she was offering her best to the eyes of all. And those with eyes to see it, well, they gave something back. Just for the sight. For the joy and the beauty of it. But that's not enough for Heron. She wanted to hook you like a fish, beauty for bait. Just as Bird had hooked me, with his bird-man and then his pies.

I waited three more days until we had a free morning, no weaving to do. After breakfast I headed for the bakery. I was afraid Heron would stop me, or at least question where I was going. But she watched me leave silently.

I took some seeds to offer. You go to someone's workplace, you make a gift to them. Over the doorway of almost every bakery is a picture of a stalk of wheat, which is also the year between Vulture and Sun, and seeds of all sorts were a proper offering for Wheat. Because of this, a strange garden had grown up in front of the bakery, where the gifts of many others like me had taken root and sprouted. Wheat, flowers, herbs, plants I could not identify, they all grew there in a tangled mass. In the same way, people will leave spiders with us when they find one in their home or at work.

I dropped my seeds on the wild garden by the gatepost and went into the bakery. The smell made me hungry. A round woman of average height stood behind the counter. She must have made the pies. I could tell she knew who I was as soon as I walked through the door. *So,* I thought. *This is Bird's mother, maybe?*

I went right to her and handed her the bag that had held the pies. She looked at it, then at me. I could see her confusion, could almost hear her mind turning over, trying to find words. So I spoke instead.

"Your pies were wonderful."

"Thank you," she said, "but I didn't make them. Bird, my boy. He did. It's my recipe, though."

So she was his mother. And baker boy had made the pies after all. At least a gift from his own hands and his own work was a little bit easier to set beside my name. I looked around the room. The walls were dark wood, and there were shelves filled with all sorts of breads: dark loaves, light loaves, braided loaves, flat loaves, rolls, biscuits, and things

I couldn't name. The warm and spicy smell of sweet baking things was over all of it. I wondered where Bird was.

All this time his mother was watching me, silent, not really comfortable with me being there for some reason. I thought to pull her tail a little.

"Bird, is he here? I have something for him."

She stiffened, started to speak, but before she could get a word out, Bird appeared. He must have been listening. He came through a door behind the counter and stood next to his mother.

"You see, Ma, I told you people would follow the pies here. The gift comes back."

You're right about that, I thought, *but maybe not like you think.*

"The gift has come back, I think from someplace close, hasn't it?" she said, looking at him as if he had done something wrong.

I wondered what I had walked into, or eaten my way into.

"Ma. She showed me such beautiful things, I had to give them to her. Besides, I bet she gave most of them away herself and they're in people's stomachs all over town."

Now they were talking about me as if I wasn't even there. And then I felt shame at Bird's words because I had kept and eaten all the pies. Not one to Heron, not one to Aster. I had not let the gift move, no. I had eaten it myself. Serves me right for giving up my name.

"I heard you say you had something for me. Can you show me?" Bird came out from behind the counter and stood in front of me. Brown hair, blue eyes, and a dusting of flour all over him.

"Of course I can. Come with me."

His mother did not look happy with this.

"Bird. You come back quick, hear? We have work to do, and your place is here."

I turned, went out the door, and Bird followed. We walked down the road in the sun. It was bright and clear, the morning still young. A few people passed on foot or on bicycles, but mostly we were alone. I knew he was waiting for me to speak, but I wouldn't. *Let him wonder.* We walked past the gate to Heron's, and I saw his surprise when we didn't go in. *Where is she taking me?* he must have been thinking. Well. He would find out soon enough. Past Heron's is a produce stand where you can get fruits and vegetables for the midday meal and dinner. We weavers often got food from there. I stepped up to the window.

"Path, I don't usually see you in the morning," said the sad man who was always there. His name was Coral.

"I know. Can I have one orange melon, please?"

"Sure. Here you go."

He handed me the fruit. I would be back later with something to trade in return.

"Okay now, Bird, we go this way." I led him across the

scrub grass by the vegetable stand and came to the path to the beach. All the way to the edge of the water we went, and there I sat him down.

"A fine gift you gave me, all those pies, and how am I to return it? I have thought about this, Bird, and I will show you something no one has ever seen before. No one. Ever. But you must close your eyes."

He did as he was told. Quickly, I took my knife and cut the melon in two. Holding one half in each hand, I told him he could look again.

"See, Bird. The inside of this melon. No one has seen that. But now you. And me." Without a word he took one of the halves from me, bit a piece of the flesh, chewed, and swallowed. Some of the juice ran down his chin.

"Path, I've used that one before. It's an old, old trick. But maybe not so old where you come from. But you are right, also. No one has seen this before. And the melon is really good."

He looked at me over the melon, and I took a bite of the other half. It was good. But Coral's fruit always is.

We sat and ate a while in silence. I gave him my knife to scoop the seeds out of the middle of the melon. Finally he spoke.

"I gave you the pies because I wanted you to notice me. I hoped you would like them and think that I could do something interesting and special like you."

"Like me?"

"Like you." He paused, chewing. Chewing his thoughts, too. "When I saw you over at the Weavers' Yard, it was like nothing I'd ever seen. Because you seemed to be alive in what you were doing. So interested in everything about the cloth. So happy in what you were doing."

"I seem that way?"

"You do. When you are working, you look alive to the tips of your fingers. And you are always doing something beautiful. When you dipped your hands in the dye and let it run down your arms, it was the most wonderful thing I have ever seen. And you did that for me. That was beauty there. So maybe I made the pies for you because I hoped I could become a little like you when I made them, like I could feel something of me going into the work, and not just the same thing over and over."

I didn't know what to say. Bird, moved by me? Wanting to be like me? No one would want to be like me. Not if they knew the truth. I held the Sun and Moon tight, willing away the sadness and tears.

10

Bird

She was holding something in her hands. It was some sort of pendant and hung from a piece of yarn around her neck.

"What is that?" I asked.

"Oh. Nothing. Something from home," she said.

"Where is home?"

"I'm from the mountains. From Boon. We raised sheep, and I learned to weave from the weavers there. But my mother . . ." She stopped, swallowed hard, and went on. "My mother was a dancer. From Rollydee. And she was so beautiful. When I think of beauty, when I feel the thread and color run through my hands, it's her I feel. But she's gone now."

All this time, she held the little pendant, clutching it hard, her knuckles white.

"Is this from your mother?" I asked.

"Oh, yes. It was hers."

"Can I see it?"

At first I thought she wouldn't let me, but slowly, one at a time, she opened her fingers and held it out to me. It was small, a little bigger around than my thumb. It had two faces. On one side was the moon, silver inlaid over a black stone. On the other side was the sun, gold over rose quartz. "Sun and Moon," she said.

She fell silent, and I waited for her to speak.

"Do you know the story of Sun and Moon's daughter?"

"Tell me," I said. I did know the story but wanted to go where the telling would take her.

"It was my mother's favorite story. She would dance it," she said and told the story, which, as my father's child, I knew by heart.

Sun and Moon, having known each other for a long time, decided to get married. "This will work out well," said Sun. "I have to work during the day, and you at night."

"That is right," said Moon. "We understand each other. The light and the dark."

"The night and the day," said Sun.

"What you lack I have," said Moon, high in the night sky with the stars, looking down on the world of darkness and mystery.

"And what you lack I have," said Sun, high in the noon sky, looking down on a world with scarcely a shadow in it.

"We will be happy forever," they both said.

And for a long time they were. For years and years and years. And then they decided to have a child.

When she was born, she was beautiful and unlike anything they had ever seen before. She was covered with fur of different colors. A third part of her was black as night, a third part of her was bright fiery orange with darker red stripes, and a third part of her was white as snow. Her eyes were golden with black pupils.

Her parents admired her.

"Look how bright and fiery she is," said Sun. "She is clearly my child. Bright as the day she is."

"Oh, but look at how deep black she is," said Moon. "Black as the night. Clearly she is my child."

"Oh, no," said Sun, "look again. See how bright her white fur is? Bright as my light. This is my child."

"Oh, no," said Moon. "Her white fur is the color of my own light on snow, or on the sandy beach at midnight when I am full and pulling the ocean to me."

"But Moon, look at what she does," replied Sun, getting a bit testy. "She lies in my light all day long, bathing in it. She turns over and over so that all of her gets to feel my light and warmth. And when she looks up, her eyes are bright and golden except for the tiniest slit in the middle. This is my child."

"Sun," said Moon, "look again. At night she walks and runs and jumps and plays in the dark. It is her time. And when she looks up, her eyes are huge black circles. Black as night with just a tiny ring of gold around them. Surely you can see that she is my child."

"No," said Sun, "she is mine."

"She is mine," said Moon.

Sun and Moon got so mad they barely spoke to each other. And then Bear came to them in a dream to give their child a name, as Bear always does. Usually Bear will tell the child's name to its mother. But she knew Sun would never believe Moon if she told him the name, so she came to both of them and gave them the same dream. In the dream she said: "Sun and Moon, you are both foolish. This child is not the daughter of Sun, and she is not the daughter of Moon. She is the child of both of you, and she belongs to herself. She has all your light and all your darkness and many more things all her own that you cannot know except by knowing her. Be thankful. She is a great gift to you. Her name is Cat."

And Sun and Moon woke from their dream and told their daughter her name.

"Daughter," said Moon, "Bear has come to us in a dream and told us your name."

"I know," said Cat.

"Your name is Cat," said Sun.

"I know," said Cat.

"You are not my daughter," said Moon.

"You are not my daughter," said Sun.

"You are the daughter of us both," they said.

"I know," said Cat.

"And a gift to us both," said Sun and Moon. "The gift moves."

"It moves," said Cat. And she leaped for joy, high into the air, landing as always squarely on her feet, and ran through the world, up and down trees, in and out of shadows, and then lay down to sleep for half the day. And that is the story.

When she finished, I asked, "And your mother?"

"She would dance the part of Cat. And the Cat Dance, where Cat leaps up for joy, that was her favorite part. And her name, too."

"What was her name?"

"Cat Sign."

"What happened to her?"

"She's gone."

"I'm sorry."

"I used to miss her so much. There was nothing like her in Boon. She could make things happen just by moving. She was like a bright light, and when she shined on me I felt like I was the only one. Special. When I was little she would pick me up and dance the Cat Dance, holding me high in the air. And when she was gone the light was gone."

And with those words she ran into the ocean. Not the way you run into the surf when you are going to swim. She ran the way you would run if you were planning to jump off a cliff and were afraid you wouldn't have the courage to go through with it if you had time to look down when you got to the edge.

I followed her into the water. "Path! Path!" Calling her name because I couldn't see her. I looked around, afraid she would drown, and then she was beside me, swimming.

"The sea helps. Sometimes. I am clean, new, and I can start over."

I thought about that. It looked to me as if she'd thrown herself in the sea in search of an end and not a beginning. I put that in my mind beside my memory of her quickness and delight in her work, seeing these things together as glimpses of different sides of one thing. Or as different facets of a single, multifaceted jewel.

By this time we had begun to walk back through the surf to the beach. She looked at me then, full-on as she had the other day when she put her hands in the dye.

"There was nothing like my mother in Boon," she said. "Nothing like her in all my life with the sheep. Nothing like her until I met the weavers."

"How did you meet them?" I asked.

She turned and began to walk down the beach on dry sand, fast. I followed.

"We took our wool to the weavers in Boon every year, and the first time I went along with my father and saw the cloth they had made, looked at their bright colored yarn, watched it come shining from the dye, I saw something of my mother in it. And as soon as I saw it I wanted it."

"You wanted to weave?"

"I couldn't keep my hands off their things. The loom, the cloth, the bright yarn. It was like touching my mother, touching the thread that tied me to her. The color ran in my hands, and I thought: *this will take me to you. I will learn to do this.*"

"And that is how you came to the cloth?"

"That's how. And it took me here, finally."

"I'm glad it took you here," I said.

"It keeps taking me," she said.

"How?"

"I guess I thought that working with Heron would be like having my mother back. Because she is so good at what she does and there is so much beauty in it. But it's not. Heron pushes me and I do things. Things that scare me. I'm afraid I'll hurt myself or someone else."

I remembered the dye running down her arms, bright blue and blood red.

"Bird, when I put the dye on my hands and showed myself to you that way, I was taking a chance. That dye is not good to touch, it can hurt your skin and your insides. It could have hurt me then if Heron hadn't got it off for me. And the thing is, when I did it I knew and I didn't care."

"You didn't care about hurting yourself?"

"No. And when Heron saw what I had done, she approved of it. Of taking the risk. She told me I was pulling the web."

"She said that?" Pulling the web was not a thing to be thought of lightly, much less done without reverence and need. Spider holds us all, and we do well to tread lightly in the world she has woven for us.

Path went on. "Heron said she was made lame by working with the dye. That she had pulled the web, and her staff was her reward. She said I would pull the web, too. And sometimes I'm afraid she's right. When I'm closest to the cloth and the color, I'm afraid she's right."

"Heron? She'd probably pull Spider's leg if she thought she could get close enough."

"Or get someone to pull it for her."

By now we were almost dry, and I knew I was going to be very late coming back to the bakery and Ma and my sister. But I couldn't leave Path.

"Do you want to stay here a while?" I asked.

"No. Thanks. I should go. You, too, from what I can tell of your ma."

"Yeah. She'll be mad."

"She doesn't like me, does she?"

"I don't know." I hedged, wanting to be loyal.

"Oh yes you do. And I know, too. The Hand at the Weavers'. Who is from far away and who will go back there. Who will distract her good son from his good work and his good life and good future, and then, when he's good and confused, her time will be up and she'll be gone for good. That about cover it?"

"Well. Yes. It does," I said. "But I don't feel that way. I was glad you told me what you did. About yourself and your work. And your own way." We had reached the gate to the Weavers' Yard, and she stopped, touched me for the first time—on the arm.

"Thank you, Bird. Thank you for listening to me. And for following me into the water."

"I was glad to. I want to see you again. Can we go someplace, sometime?"

"When I can get away from Heron. And when you can get away from your ma."

Then she was gone. I turned and walked down the street, steeling myself for the storm that would break on my head when I walked into the bakery.

My mother and Crystal must have seen me coming, for they were waiting behind the counter, mouths set in identical frowns as I walked through the door.

I waited, determined not to speak first. I could always outwait my mother and sister, and I knew that if I let Ma begin, things would go easier. But it was a very heavy silence. And long. Long enough to count the dust motes and flour grains floating in the sunlight. Long enough to begin to worry. I wished the cat would come through and say something just to break the silence. But no. No sound, not even the tick of a heating oven. I was beginning to consider breaking the silence myself when my mother spoke.

"Bird. This has gone far enough."

Her voice was angry and sad at the same time, and I wished I had not given her pain.

"Your life and your time are yours. You know that. But not yours alone. You, Crystal, and me, we have a life together, and we do our part in it, or everything suffers. Everything. There is a lot of work to do here, every day, and when you leave without doing your part, then your sister and I have to make up for it." Here she paused and looked at Crystal, who nodded. "When two must do the work of three, it suffers. The work suffers. We suffer. The people who will eat what we bake suffer because even if in their hunger they do not know it, what they are receiving from us is not our best. And Bird, even you suffer because we are all connected."

Here I could sense Spider creeping into the conversation and wished she would creep away. I had heard enough of her already.

"Bird, you are so good with what you do. At least as good as me and Crystal, maybe better. Certainly it would be better if you stayed here and were steady instead of going off all the time. If you're not off traveling on the island somewhere, you're traveling in your mind. You want to work with your hands, and what do you do? You sculpt little figures from clay. Use those hands on the dough, on what we have together. What we have here."

I knew she was winding down now, nearing the end, and that some sort of punishment or sanction was coming.

"So what we have decided, decided in all the leisure time we had after doing all your work as well as ours, is this: tomorrow the bakery is yours. We will do what you say, but only what you say. Only what you plan and oversee will be done. If you leave, daydream, get lazy, then work will stop. If you stay and keep on top of things, then what you choose will happen."

This was not what I had expected, and I sensed something new in my mother, a different way of seeing me, of being with me. But I knew when to seize the initiative and run.

"All right. If that is what you want, that is what we will do. I will make up a list of what we need for tomorrow, and we'll see what we have and what we'll have to go out and get." Meat pies, I was thinking. That would be something unusual, a different smell in the street for the hungry nose. And something chocolate, too. I found paper and pen and set to work, looking through cupboards and coolers to see what we had on hand.

Walset, the cat, found me in the back room. "Where were you when I needed you, huh?"

"Smell," he said, pushing his head into my hand and

then sniffing my leg and pants. "Ocean. Fish." Then he marked my ankle with the scent glands in his jaw. Once, twice. "Walset," he said, naming his own scent he had just placed on me. He left, tail high.

I wondered why my mother had not asked anything about where I had been. I knew she was concerned and that she didn't think Path was the sort of person I ought to spend time with. But she said not a word about it. In a way, she seemed to accept where I had been but was upset with my having missed work. Her words alone might make me think she didn't care whether I saw Path or not. But I knew better. With my mother there is always more than words, and the part she didn't say was often more important than the part she did say. And it was up to her to bring the unspoken part out and up to me to wait for it to come.

But this left me troubled. Because if she had brought up Path, I could have got the conversation around to where I could have said something about what had happened with Path today. What she had said and done. And I could have tried to explain why I stayed gone for so long—that I was afraid of what Path would do if I left. I thought about saying something but feared my mother's anger, since she had decided the subject was off-limits.

So that afternoon, while making dough for the evening's baking, I spoke to Crystal about Path.

"Crystal, have you heard anything about the girl from the Weavers'? The new Hand? Path is her name."

"You're asking me? You, who watch the Weavers' Yard every chance you get?"

Was I really that obvious? I wondered.

"No, Crystal, I mean, do you know anyone who knows her, who talks with her? Any of the girls." Crystal was older than me and had many friends, and they all met and talked often. "I'm serious, Crystal. I worry about her."

This surprised her, and she looked at me for a moment.

"No. Not really. Though I have asked about her, because Ma . . ." She thought better of finishing that sentence, but what she said told me that my mother was concerned. She went on. "They say that she seems busy and tired. She will come around to get things the weavers need but won't talk much. And Robin over at the carvers' said she had tried to ask her about her home and how she came to be with Heron. But she wouldn't say. She was polite and nice, Robin said, but wouldn't talk about herself. And you know that Heron doesn't like any of the weavers to mingle much. Anyway, Bird, she just got here. She hasn't really had time to meet anyone."

I decided to take the plunge. "If I tell you something, will you not tell anybody?"

"Of course, Bird."

"Because this is what Path told me. Her gift in the telling. It is not really mine to tell. But I don't know what to do."

"Bird, I won't tell anyone. I promise."

"Crystal, the reason I was so late is that I was afraid."

"Of what?"

"Afraid she would hurt herself."

"Why?"

"Because she said that was what scared her. Because her mother is gone, dead, I guess, from what she said. Because she is all alone with nothing except her work, and it is dangerous sometimes. Because, look, she threw herself in the ocean, and I thought she wanted to drown."

"You know what Ma would say to that?"

"What?"

"She would say that girl was no good to you, that a drowning person is always trying to pull under the people who would save her."

And she was right. I could hear Ma saying that.

"But if it's any help, I don't feel that way. I think that girl—Path?—I think she's lonely and away from everything familiar, and she doesn't have friends and is afraid. Heron is not an easy person to be with even for a little while. It would be hard to look forward to spending every day with her for five years."

"Yeah. I wonder what it's like over there. What they do when they're not busy."

"I think they're always busy. Do they ever come over here? Well, except for this morning, maybe once a month. Once a month Heron will show up for some bread, rolls, something. But it's as if she's doing it in a formal way, not as a part of things."

"I bet she does that with every bakery, every market, every everything. Wants us all to remember she was in, re-member her face passing through. But no connection, no back-and-forth."

"Yes," Crystal said. "Distant."

And then we got on with the baking. But that night I thought about my talk with Crystal. About how it helped me come back to myself after what had happened with Path that morning. I knew then what I would do when I had the chance, when I could get away after my day of running the bakery. I would go see my father.

11

Path

When I got back to Heron's, I went through the rest of the work in a daze. We got the cloth under cover, all dry now, the dye set. I checked the supplies for the next day, tested the color in the dye vat, shut down the fires, and went to our tent.

I lay on my mat on the floor, too tired to undress. The soft sea sound came through the cloth, breathing in and out. *You could have taken me away today,* I thought. *I wanted it. I wanted it, just for a moment.*

Bird. Why had I talked to him? What was in me became real when I gave it words and gave the words to him. But where would the words take me if I let all of them out? If I could keep quiet I could keep safe.

* * *

The next day I worked as hard and long as I could so that I would fall asleep at night without having to think.

Even Heron noticed. "Path, you will outrun the power loom if you go any faster. What is chasing you?" she asked.

What was chasing me was inside me, and I was running as fast as I could just to stay in one place. And it worked. For four days.

On the fifth day Heron woke me early in the morning.

"Path. Path." She was carrying a big bundle of cloth, tightly wrapped in black. "Wake up. There is much for you to do today. You must take this where it is to go."

I sat up and looked at the bundle, still sleepy.

"Girl, these are the robes for Sun and Moon. Look."

She undid the cord that held the bundle and showed me the cloth inside. It was like nothing I had ever seen before. The gold of the sun was brighter than any cloth I had seen, and the silver of the moon was cool as night, with a tiny bit of blue to hint at the mystery of the dark and the things that move in it.

"What do you think of that, eh? These hands have a few surprises for you yet, girl. You will walk with beauty today, and everyone will know, even though it is hidden."

She held the cloth as if it was part of herself. She held it the way a beautiful woman holds her body when she wants her beauty to be seen.

"Where do you want me to take it?"

"Oh, Path. When you take this up, you are taking your place in the story we weave for the turning of the year. You are a strand in the cloth now, and your strand goes to the Circle. When you need to know where to go from there, you will know. Believe that."

This sounded strange to me. Was I supposed to wander around until someone came up to me and said, "Oh, yes, that's mine, thank you"?

She saw my confusion, and the corners of her mouth turned up a little. *As close as you'll get to a smile,* I thought. But she would tell me no more. "Just keep this close and do not let anyone see it. Sun and Moon, these are the colors that turn night and day. No one should look at them before their proper time and place on Midsummer Day. But when they do look"—she held me with her gaze—"they will know the cloth is ours. They will not care who wears the robes made from what you carry, who walks as Sun, who walks as Moon. But they will always remember the wonder of what they see, and that it came from our hands.

"'Look,' they'll say when they pass one of us in the street, 'they made the cloth for Sun and Moon.'" Her eyes flashed power and pride. She strode out of the tent and I followed her.

"Sun and Moon walk one day, girl, but you and I, we

will walk every day. People will see us at our work today, tomorrow, next week, and everyone will know the beauty of what we did. Everyone. This is part of your way in the cloth. To be seen carrying the thing no one may see. They will see you and remember. Now go. Back before the sun is down."

I nodded and watched her leave, heading for the loom-house with more work for Aster.

I went to the sea to bathe, then put on fresh clothes and picked up the bundle of cloth. Then I headed out of the yard, into the street, and past the bakery. The wonderful smell was there as always, and Bird somewhere inside. I stopped and felt my hunger. I could go in, just for some bread. Everybody has to eat. Maybe someone there would tell me where to take the cloth. I stood by the doorway and then made myself enter. Inside, there were quite a few people, picking up loaves, laughing, arguing with Bird's ma about what they would trade for her wares. Then I saw a girl behind the counter who looked just like Bird's mother. *The sister,* I thought. *Older.* She looked at me and smiled. She glanced at her mother then, saw that she was busy, and motioned for me to come closer.

"You're Path, aren't you, from the Weavers'?"

"Yes. I am."

"I am Crystal. Bird is my brother."

"I could tell. You look like your mother."

"Yes. Everybody says." She looked down at the shelves

of bread, then said, "You take what you want. You must be hungry."

"If I take a whole loaf, what would you take in return?"

"Path, if you would give me a cloth to wear on my head, something bright to keep my hair out of the dough, something pretty that people will remember, then you can take thirteen loaves."

"Done," I said. "Do you like red and yellow?" I was thinking of the last batches of cloth we had made and knew there were enough leftover pieces to make what she wanted many times over. "I will bring it tomorrow. And can I get my thirteen loaves over time, or do I have to take them all at once?"

"Anytime you want," she said.

"Then I will take two now and the rest later." I picked the loaves of bread. They were firm and crackly on the outside and smelled ever so slightly of smoke.

"Those are from the wood oven," Crystal said. "They have a little taste of the fire in them."

"They do. I can smell it." I hesitated, then asked her, "Is Bird here?"

She looked again at her mother to see if she was watching. But her mother was still joking and bargaining with a big sunburned man across the room. *Fisherman?* I wondered. Satisfied, Crystal turned to me.

"No," said Crystal. "He's gone to visit our father. But when he comes back, I'll tell him you were here."

"Thank you," I said.

"And Path. Come back soon. You'll have to get the rest of your loaves."

"And bring your head cloth."

I turned to leave and saw a large tiger cat come in through the front door. He looked at me, saw I was new to him, and walked up to smell my offered hand. "Path," I said, scratching his chin. He then marked my ankles with his scent—head and tail both. "Path," he said back to me, and then "Walset," his own name.

"He likes you," Crystal said as I reached the door.

I walked down the street wondering where the cloth was to go. I broke off a piece of the bread and chewed. It was good, better than anything I had eaten since coming to Heron's except Bird's pies. I would go to the Circle, I thought. I could ask someone where to go from there. I had not been long with Heron, but I already knew that she seldom gave me a task whose results were obvious. She had sent me to deliver the cloth, and I knew I would find more questions than answers along the way.

I passed houses and workshops built far enough from the beach to have some protection from storms. The island was a beautiful place, I thought. And there seemed to be people everywhere doing something. I passed a house where a group of small children were singing along with the radio as they ran, played in the yard, and walked in and out of the house. In fact, the radio was everywhere, soft sounds of talk and songs coming through windows or from radios people had set outdoors where they worked or sat.

I remembered that the radio was always playing in the bakery, too. Not at Heron's. I had never heard the radio there. Didn't even know if she had one. Beauty and the cloth were what counted for her, and everything else just had to wait. I thought of the heavy bundle I carried and what she had told me about it.

People would be wearing the cloth I carried. They would walk as Sun and Moon on Midsummer Day. This was like the Midsummer Days I knew from Boon. Everyone would come down from the hills with some of the sheep, always leaving a few cousins behind to tend the rest of the flock, and gather at the Circle. The other clans from nearby would come, and there would usually be some travelers, away from home for some reason. They would sing the songs and dance the dances—though not so many songs as they sang here, with the radio going all the time. The Years would walk, all thirteen of them. People would eat until they had eaten too much, drink until they had drunk too much, pass around gifts and sheep and wool and fish and whatever else they had. Couples would disappear into the woods for a while, then reappear and join the feast again.

And when the sun came up and it was over, my family would go back up the valley to home and flocks minus some sheep and all the gifts they had given to the fire.

Everyone but me. I had not been to the Circle at Midsummer Day since my mother had brought me back to Boon. When the time came to go to the Circle, I would run and hide. Running and hiding are things I do very well.

The radio kept playing one or another of the Turning Songs and plenty of new ones that I hadn't heard before. And people sang them at their work, at home, in the street, sometimes right along with the radio and sometimes just by themselves, with whatever voice and tune they could manage. Just now a man was pushing a cart full of dried fish down the street ahead of me, singing:

> All things come when they are called,
> If you know the words to say,
> All things come when they are called,
> If you know the words to say,
> All things come when they are called,
> If you know the words to say.

I wondered where the cloth I carried would go, who would wear it. I turned away from the sea and up the street that led to the Circle. As I approached, I could see that it was crowded with people, all of them busy building stands, putting up tents, nailing, lifting. The fire pit was full of kindling—big logs and several whole trees. Radios were playing everywhere, and I tried to shut the whole thing out. I had no idea where I was supposed to go and felt like a fool. Head down, I walked across the Circle and watched the tattooed circle by my big toe go up and down with my steps. I didn't see the man come up to me, didn't know he was there until he touched my arm. I jumped.

"Weaver girl," he said.

"What do you want?"

"You, of course, and what you're carrying. I'll show you where it goes."

He was tall, with dark hair. He put down his hammer and nails and led me back across the Circle.

"Where are we going?" I asked.

"To Sun Came's place," he replied. "She's been waiting for you."

So this is what Heron meant when she told me I was stepping into the story, into the cloth. This was why she would not tell me where I was to go. Sun Came, who was she? And where? I felt I had as much control over my life as the thread in a loom, rushing back and forth with the shuttle to make a pattern that thread can never see. Found by this man with the hammer, I felt lost again, like I had by the sea with Bird. What I carried, beautiful as it was, would not let me go.

12

Bird

Everybody knows my father. Of course, everybody here knows everybody in some way, but with my father it is different. People hear him all the time. His voice is a presence in the town—telling stories, asking questions, explaining, remembering, reminding. He runs the radio station. And he is a Year, which complicates everything.

There are thirteen Years, and each one has a name and each one is a person. They have names because each year is a piece of life, a step around the spiral that you will make as you live your life. And each year is a person, too, because the spirit of that year has work to do, and if it's going to get done, somebody has to do it. It's an honor to be chosen as a Year, to wear your robes and walk with the other Years in the Circle on Midsummer Day. But it can get complicated. Everyone knows you as two people, yourself and your year. Sometimes, like with the Vultures, it can be hard to see the person for the year.

Being a Year means a lot of work. Sun and Moon are midwives and come when babies are born. Fish, Cat, and Turtle will teach you about what is inside you in the places you can't see. Cat will show you the night, Fish will show you about water, change, and flow, and Turtle has her shell for protection and for when you need to be alone. During your life you'll spend some time with all three of them, first as a child, then as an adult, and finally when you are old. Lizard gives you your tattoo when you stop being a child and start to be an adult. I had got mine a year ago: a big brown bird with a bright yellow beak, open and pointing at my heart. There is Snake the healer, Bear who gives you dreams, Rabbit who plays jokes on everybody, and the Vultures who come when you die. Wheat is in charge of the Midsummer Day festival because wheat is what falls into the ground to die and live again. And Ant is in charge of work done for the common good, like building things and repairing roads and docks. For the next weeks, right up to Midsummer Day, Ant and Wheat would be very busy. And there's one Year left to tell about, Spider, who weaves the stories and songs that make up the web, who is also my father.

And I, his son, sometimes feel I don't know him any better than anyone else. He's the familiar voice in the air. Common property, even. Not mine in a special way. Every dad. Universal dad. But I knew that I could get past that when I went to see him. His public voice would fall away, and, after a while, we would be father and son together. And we could talk.

From what Crystal had told me I knew that my mother had spoken to him about Path. I thought that if I sought him out, I could tell him about Path and why I was afraid for her. That way I could get my side of things into the discussion before my father and mother got together and made decisions for me. One of those talks between the two of them had kept me in the bakery all year. I didn't want that to happen again, not if I could do anything about it.

To get to the radio station you must go all the way to the Circle and then turn inland toward the Sound. Up ahead of me I could see Ant and Wheat walking along, deep in talk. Not in their robes, of course. Years wear their robes only on Midsummer Day, except for the Vultures, who also wear them whenever they tend the dead. They turned in to the Circle, and I went on my way. As you get close to the Sound, the ground rises a little. The radio station was put there so that it would be less likely to be lost in a storm with a big tidal surge and lots of waves and wind. There was always talk of moving it closer to the ocean, so that the sea could take it when it wanted. But people valued the radio for providing storm warnings and felt there was no reason to lose the station to the thing it was supposed to warn us of. Besides, they said, if the sea really wanted it, the sea would take it. The sea had covered the entire town once in living memory and taken many buildings, though not the radio station.

This had happened before I was born, but stories about rejoicing and rebuilding after the storms were told all the time. All the time. I remembered my father talking to old Sandpiper, famous for having run out the front door of his house as the sea took it from the back.

"So, Sandpiper," my father had asked, deep into his radio self now, "when did you know your house was going?"

"Why, when the pilings cracked and broke and the sea came in the back door. Crack! Crash! Bang! Bang! And water everywhere. I ran out the front door, singing the Giving Song as I went. I ran up the street in the wind and watched it go, just like a Ship on the waves."

And of course the next thing my father did was play a recording of the Giving Song and got Sandpiper to sing along.

> What I have I give
> To what is larger,
> What is next,

What is passing through,
Passing on.
Go now, go now, go now.

And then, when the song was over, he got him to tell the story again. While all the town was listening to the radio. For the millionth time. This is what drives me crazy. Yes, we do mean this. We do rejoice in giving, even in the taking of what we had not planned to give. But why do we have to hear about it over and over? I get the idea. I got it a long time ago.

I could see the tower of the radio station through the trees, then I came into the clearing where my father's house and workshop stood, the shed with the fuel cell. This was an unusual place. For one thing, about half of all the metal in town was there, between the tower and the hydrogen tank for the emergency fuel cell. We kept it so the radio could stay on all night if need be, in an emergency or a storm, so it could stay on if the wind took the battery tree that charged the batteries. This had never happened in my lifetime, and people grumbled about keeping the machinery just as they grumbled about moving the radio station closer to the beach. But they never did anything about it. They liked the radio. They liked my father.

He was not born here on the Banks but had come from

far away, the M'ssippi Valley. His family were hunter-gatherers who roamed over a large area on both sides of the river. When he was given his name, How the Wind Goes, he took a solitary journey to learn its meaning. He came all the way to the Banks and never left. And then he met my mother. But that is another story.

And there he was, standing in the doorway to greet me. Tall, with black hair and a long beard. He was wearing bright yellow drawstring pants and nothing else.

"Where he flies, what he sees, Bird Speaks, and speaks to me." Sometimes he talked in rhyme, the way his people did. I answered him the same way.

"How the Wind Goes, what he knows."

He came out and hugged me. "Bird," he said.

"Dad."

"I thought you might be coming here today."

"You did?" Maybe he and Ma had been talking more than I thought.

"Yes. Come on in. I have to say a few things to the town, and then we can talk a while."

I followed him into the little control room. It was always the same, the clutter and piles of stuff. Shells, feathers, bones, and dried leaves were everywhere. There was a big window looking out on the trees. He sat by the window in front of the microphone and turned it on when the recording ended. He settled into a story, this one about Midsummer Day last Rabbit year when the fire wouldn't light because of the rain. A thousand people standing around naked in the wet earnestly talking about the need to give the fire to the rain while trying to figure out how to get rid of clothes if they couldn't burn them. And he was right. It was funny. I had been there. And what else would you expect from Rabbit, who always plays tricks on you?

Dad's cat, Twelve, lay on the floor by the door. I bent to pet her.

"Bird," she said, sniffing my hand and starting to purr. She stood up and paraded around my ankles, smelling and marking at the same time.

"Twelve. Walset. Walset."

Our cat, Walset, had come from Twelve's litter that Rabbit year, and she always seemed to like him. And vice versa. Sometimes he would fall asleep kneading with his paws and saying her name under his breath. You had to listen hard to hear it, but that's what he said. Cats. I picked Twelve up and put her on the table in the control room next to my father, who had just finished his story about the rained-out fire and started a recording of all the fire dance music. It would take an hour to finish.

"So, Bird. What brings you here?"

He was attentive and out of his public self all at once. *A good sign*, I thought. "Well, I wanted to talk to you. About this girl."

"It's time for you to think about girls, that's true enough. You were born in Vulture year and have come all around the circle, and now your second Vulture year will end. Who is she?"

"She lives at the Weavers' Yard with Heron. She is her new Hand. I've met her across the fence, and have talked to her and—"

"You've given her things, yes? Started the back-and-forth?"

"Well, yes, we have. I mean, it's not like I am really serious, but I wanted to do what was right. I didn't know her."

"No, of course not. Though I must say, Bird, that you are always serious. Especially when you're not being serious. But she is new here, not somebody you have played with, not somebody you have eaten with and whose mother and father and brother you know. So you had to start in the formal way."

"Yes. And she and I talked, and what she said scares me. And I don't know what to do about it." I could tell this surprised him; it was not what he was expecting to hear.

"Tell me," he said, "what did this girl say to you?"

"She said she was frightened. And I am frightened for her."

"How?"

So I told him everything, right up to her jumping into the ocean, with me right behind her.

"Well," he said. "What do you think is going to happen?"

"I don't know. She said that her work was dangerous and that she would take chances. When she put her hands in the dye, that was taking a chance. It could have hurt her, and she didn't know how to get it off. Heron got it off for her."

"I bet old Heron gave her a talking-to over that," he said.

"No. She didn't. Heron encouraged her. She told Path that she was the sort to pull on the web. Heron said that she'd got her lame leg and staff from pulling the web. Said that it was worth it. Said she'd do it again. Said Path would, too."

"Pulling on the web. I will show you something about that." He led me outside into the trees by the house and tower. He showed me the web of a big garden spider hanging between the lower branches of the trees. The web was almost three feet across, and the gold and black spider's body was bigger than my thumb. He pointed to the web. "Pull on this web and Spider comes, if she is interested. And if you have pulled hard enough to get stuck in the web, she will bite you and you will sleep. You will not die. You will sleep. And she will spin more silk, wrap you in it, and put you away, like them." He pointed to a couple of shiny capsules of silk attached to the outer bands of the web. "They are food for later on. They sleep. Their bodies live, they breathe. But they cannot move. They cannot leave.

They are stuck in the moment that Spider bit them. Reliving that moment over and over, maybe. Bound to the web, not connected by it. That is what you can get if you pull the web hard enough. Maybe there is something like that in Path. Something of her mother frozen in her."

"She wouldn't tell me much about her mother. Just that she was a dancer and that she was gone."

My father thought for a minute. "If Path is looking for what a mother can give, she won't find it with Heron. She wants love, and Heron is going to give her work and art and then demand that she produce cloth in return. You know, old Heron is a different sort of person. I think she would have been happier in the Old Time when she could have been rich. When she could have had piles of things."

"How do you mean?"

"I mean that no one can keep a lot of things now. People would look down on you. But there are other ways to be rich. And I think this is what she does. She wants to build up her riches in people's minds, in their estimation of her, but through her work alone. And sure, that is something everybody does, by doing work well or by giving in an artful and memorable way. You with your pies for Path. That sort of thing."

He started to walk in a circle around the radio tower, and I followed him.

"But for Heron it is different. The cloth is her self. It sounds like she wants Path to become like her."

"Like Heron? How? Heron is old and unfriendly."

"Is Path friendly?" he asked. "It sounds like sometimes she wants to be but doesn't know how. She needs to learn. She needs friends, Bird. She needs you."

We walked back into the house, where the Fire Songs were still going strong.

"You know," my father said, "there has always been something different about Heron's Hands."

"How so?"

"They always come from far away. And often they come and go with a big load of goods. Think about this. It is proper to have some back-and-forth, some sort of gifting to accompany a Hand who has chosen to leave home to learn a craft. But I wonder if there is not more than that going on here."

"You mean that Heron trades for Hands?"

"She could. She could. And if that had happened with Path, if she felt that she had been the subject of barter and bargaining, wouldn't she feel abandoned by her people?"

"Treated as an animal, cattle, sheep."

"An animal." My father paused, weighing his words. "Of course there is no simple rule for this. No clear line where back-and-forth stops and trade begins. So Heron would claim she had done nothing improper, whatever she did."

"Maybe I can ask Path about that. If I can see her again.

You said she needed friends, needed me. So it will be all right for me to see her, won't it?"

"Yes, it is certainly all right with me. And I will talk to your mother. But remember. Path's way is her own, and it is not for you to change it or fix it. Respect that. Respect her. She has walked into a difficult place, and though it may not be the place she would have chosen, it is hers. Honor that. Honor her life, her self, and her way to her self."

"I will, Dad." The Fire Songs were winding down, and he turned to the control room to string out more words and stories for the town, carrying us all on his rope of words to Midsummer Day. I said goodbye to Twelve, who licked my hand and whispered, "Walset. Walset."

"I'll tell him you remembered him," I said, scratching her under the chin. She reached out with her paw and put her claws on my wrist as I started to leave.

"Bird," she said, turned me loose, and began to purr.

And I left, looking at the big spider in her web, wondering if all of us were Spider-bit somewhere inside. I turned down the path to the ocean and walked back to town.

13

Path

The hammer man who led me across the Circle was named Willet. The Circle was full of people, all of them busy with something, and he knew them all, stopped, talked, laughed, and went on. He had a bright, easy laugh with an edge to it, and I heard it often. We stopped by a man who was lifting posts from a wagon and setting them on the ground.

"Willet, you have found the weaver girl," he said, dropping another post on the grass.

"Yes, here she is." Turning to me he said, laughing, "And just what do you have all wrapped up there? What do you not want us to see, eh?"

I pulled the bundle closer. "Now you know I can't show you this."

They both laughed. Willet said goodbye to the man, and we walked on.

"You're new, aren't you?" he asked.

"Yes. I just got here a few weeks ago," I said.

"I thought so. But it's hard to be sure with you weavers. We hardly ever see you. Heron keeps you on a tight leash."

"You're seeing me now," I said. "And what about you? What do you do?"

"I build things all the time. I'm a carpenter and wood-worker. If I'm not working on a house, I'll help out at the boat yard when they're building a wooden boat. And I make furniture, too," he said.

"And now you're building things for Midsummer Day."

"Yes. In fact," he said, "the next thing I'm going to work on will be the weavers' stall. You want to see it?"

"Sure," I answered.

We walked past the fire pit to the other side of the Circle. He pointed to four stakes set in the ground where the corners would be next to a pile of lumber. "That's it," he said. "We have to get it finished, and then you weavers are supposed to cover it with cloth."

I stood where the middle of the stall would be and looked around. I pictured the Circle on Midsummer Day: the people, the noise, the fire. I held the Sun and Moon and promised myself I would find a place to hide. Let Heron make me come if she could find me.

"I'm ready to go now," I said. "Show me the way."

"It's just ahead," said Willet.

We made our way out of the Circle and came to a group of workshops and houses all clustered together. There was a place full of herbs and plants, the Battery House, and a large shop with a window filled with pots and pans and vessels of all sorts—ceramic, metal, plastic.

"And here we are," said Willet. "This is Sun Came's."

We went inside, and it seemed there were children everywhere, running around, playing among the wares. Five cats came to me, all swirling about my ankles and talking at once. "Path," I said, bending to pet them. I couldn't understand what they were saying. There was loud pounding from somewhere in the back.

"Sun Came fixes pots. The broken vessel comes here. Sun Came," he called. Then louder, "Sun Came!"

And there she was. A very tall, round woman came into the room. "I am Sun Came," she said.

"And I am Path. This is for you." I held out the bundle to her.

She smiled. "Oh. This is wonderful indeed." She took it from me and set it on the counter in the middle of the room. Willet left, saying goodbye as he went out the door. I waited for Sun Came to speak, but she was still, watching me. All of a sudden everything was quiet in the room. Even the children were silent. My turn to talk, I thought.

"You are Sun Came and you mend pots, yes?"

"That's right," she said.

"So what becomes of what I have brought you? Where will you take it?"

"I will take it where it will go next. With the rest of the robes of the Years. I have all of them now except for Sun and Moon's, so I expect that's what you've given me."

"It is. So you know. This is not a secret from you." Maybe she was somebody who could tell me what was happening, could see the pattern I was weaving in the cloth of my life. "This is a new and strange place to me, and I don't know what to expect. Don't know where to go."

"And you find yourself sent on an errand with no destination, and someone finds you and helps you along."

"Yes. Why?"

"Because we all must move the gift along. And walking through the Circle, carrying what you were carrying, you were the gift in our midst. Not the sign of it, but the gift itself. Of course you would be called, would find yourself on the way to where the gift must move. After all," she added, "we don't see you weavers often, so we knew you were doing something for Heron."

"But I don't want to be somebody's gift."

"What would you be, then?" she asked. She looked

straight at me. Her eyes were big and blue, and I felt held and seen all at once. I could tell she really meant it, really wanted my answer.

"I don't know what I would be," I said finally. "What I know is color and the cloth. But sometimes it just seems to come through me like it comes through the loom. And then I don't even know who I am but hands on the loom."

"You are your work," she said, very softly.

"Yes, sometimes."

"If you could make a place, the gift would move to you. It moves to the empty place. Always. When Midsummer Day comes and the Years walk through the town, and everyone comes to the Circle, it is a time for emptying ourselves. Of everything. We come with gifts in our hands, wearing our finest clothes, and we leave the Circle naked, with nothing. Even this"—she held up the bundle of cloth I had brought—"even this will go in the fire." Sun Came went on. "We do this in the round of the year. We sing Turning Songs at Midsummer because it is the time when the year ends and begins, when each night starts to get a little longer and each day a little shorter. We make much, but we free ourselves from it by giving it up."

She paused, looked at me again, hard. "Path," she said, "there is something in you, and it wants out. It will have its way, you know. Someday you will give it up."

No, I said to myself deep inside.

"Take a pot," she said and held up a large metal bowl

with a broken handle. "I can fix this, make it whole. And it will break again, and I will fix it again. We all break and mend. You, too. You have this thing deep in you, and you think that if you let it out, it will tear a hole nothing can fill. It will not. It will open a door instead."

"What kind of door?" I asked.

She didn't answer. Instead, she led me into the back room of the shop, then out through the garden and into her house. We went into a room that must have been her bedroom. She opened a cupboard in the wall, took out a long, dark brown robe, and laid it on the bed.

"Path, I had a door in me, just as you do. Here is what was on the other side of it. When Vulture walks on Midsummer Day, it is me. When one of us will no longer mend and must give up life, Vulture is there and takes the soul to the next place. There is more in the world, more than we can touch with these hands or see with these eyes." She touched her eyebrows as she spoke. "I know. I have been there and back."

"You have?" I had never spoken to anyone this way. I had seen Vulture walk with the Years. And the Vultures had come when my father's mother died, though we couldn't see them dance and sing. No one can see their masks except the dead person. You see Vulture's face only once, at the end. I looked at Sun Came's own face then. Black hair, strong eyebrows, cheeks round like most of the rest of her. She looked as if she should be playing with children. She looked like the sort of person who could pick up a crying baby and the baby would stop crying at once because she was so soft and soothing. She did not look like someone who would sing and dance herself into a trance to take a dying spirit to wherever it goes next. She could tell what I was thinking, I knew.

"You are wondering about me, aren't you?"

"Yes, I am. How did you decide to become Vulture? How did you learn it?"

"I didn't choose to be Vulture. The bird chose me. Vulture chooses whom Vulture will. I had no say. It was clear to me, just clear. And I was taught by the Vultures what I had to know. And so, today, here I am." She touched me then, lightly on the forehead. "Don't you think Spider might have chosen you? Might have reached out and placed you on the web, set you to going on your way, woven you even as you weave?"

"I think that sometimes. But then I think that if I am all Spider's, where is my self? Where is what is me? Where is my life, my way outside the cloth?"

"You'll have to make a place for it. Be empty and the gift will move to you. The thing deep in you, you know it wants out. And you hold it tight and try to cover it with beauty. So you are stuck. But if you were unstuck, your work would turn the world."

"What do you mean?" I asked.

"I mean that work is an opening of the way, that mend-

132

ing what is broken is how I can turn my hands to the turning of the world, how I can move with it, make it move.
The gift I can pass on. Becoming Vulture, well, that was an
extra thing. But it grows right out of what I do."

She held out her hands to me, simple and large, knuckles a little knobby, probably because she had hit them with
a hammer a time or two. I looked at my own hands, small
and thin and strong, saw the cloth and thread and color
slip through them, a rainbow in my mind. "But what else
is there?" I didn't realize I had spoken my thoughts aloud,
but Sun Came heard.

"Else than what?"

"Else than the cloth. Else than color and beauty. Sun
Came, when you pick up a pot and start to work, do you
see yourself in it, do you feel part of it, do you feel your
hands from the inside of the work?"

"Yes," she said, "sometimes I do."

"And that is how it is with me. Except that I go into the
work, and there is nothing else. I fall into it. I fall and fall."

She looked at me hard, thinking. I wondered what she
saw with her Vulture eyes.

"Yes," she said. "You fall and fall. You feel that there is
no end to it. You look at the cloth coming out of the loom
in front of you, and it is a road that never ends and leads
nowhere."

"How do you know that?" I asked.

"I know what I know, and I see what I see," she said.

"That is what Vulture gave me. And I see that you are two people. One person outside who weaves and does work so wonderful that Heron chose her for a Hand. And one person inside who unweaves everything the other person weaves. So that Path will stay where she is. She will not move with the gift but will keep it. Maybe she will call a friend with one hand and push him away with the other." Sun Came put out her hand and touched my Sun and Moon with one fingertip. "That's it, isn't it?" she said. "That Sun and Moon."

"You don't know," I said. I didn't want her to touch it.

"I watch you. I watch you feel it, hold it as if it is as precious as life itself. I think it is the latch on your door."

"No," I said. "It's just something from my mother."

"Maybe so. But remember: what wants out will have its way."

She led me out of her house, back across the garden, and into the workshop. There she reached into a box and brought out a tiny jar with a stopper.

"Take this," she said, handing it to me. "The gift moves."

I took the jar. "It moves," I said.

"Go ahead and open it. Smell it."

I did so, and a wonderful sweet smell came to me.

"It is a cream you can put on your skin when it is dry and itchy. You'll need it sometimes because of your work. It will make your hands feel better. It does for mine."

"Thank you. Goodbye now" was all I said.

"Goodbye, Path."

I put the jar in my bag and stepped out into the street. *Am I two people?* I wondered. *One unweaving as the other weaves?* I didn't know. But I knew Sun Came was right about the Sun and Moon. It was the latch to my door. To the day my mother left me. And when I was good enough, when I could weave cloth better even than Heron, then I could open it.

I walked back to the Circle and cut across it, past people hammering, sawing, carrying, building a whole wooden city on the open field. All this for one day. Willet waved as he saw me and I waved back. I hurried down the road to Heron's then, hoping no one would call to me from the bakery. I went into the tent, put away my loaves for later, placed Sun Came's jar of cream on my chest, and changed into my dye clothes. The ones splattered with little bits of all the colors I had worked with. Then I went out into the yard to take up the cloth.

14

Bird

I got back to the bakery late that afternoon. After what my father had said, I felt my worst fears for Path were true. That she really was in trouble, drowning all the time she thought she was swimming. And what to do about it? "Be her friend," my father had said. Well, how? Wait for her to talk, and risk waiting too long? Or try to get her to talk myself, and risk pushing her away? I fell asleep full of worry and was no wiser in the morning.

The next day passed as they all do, Ma and Crystal and I mixing, kneading, baking, handing out loaves and cakes and sweet things to all the people who came through. Laughing, talking, singing with the radio, or listening to my father talk and talk. But everything was moving faster. It was a busy time, right before Midsummer Day. And I felt it, too. But I was only half present. The rest of me thought about Path. When I had the chance and Ma was away, I told Crystal about talking to Dad.

"What did you say?" she asked.

"I told him about Path, how she threw herself in the ocean. About her mother, who is gone and who she won't talk about. And I told him Heron wanted Path to pull the web."

"And?"

"He took me outside the radio station and showed me a spider in her web. He said that pulling the web was a dangerous thing. He said that when a real spider's web is pulled by an insect, the spider will come and bite the insect to paralyze it, then wrap it up in silk to eat later."

"Did he mean Path was like that?"

"I think he meant that something was frozen, stuck inside her like the paralyzed bugs in the spider's web."

"So what are you going to do?" Crystal asked.

"I don't know. I'm afraid that if I go to her, talk to her, she'll run away, be silent. And I'm afraid that if I wait, I'll wait too long and something will happen. That she'll hurt herself."

"You like her, don't you, Bird?"

"Yes."

"You know, she came in yesterday while you were gone and traded me a headscarf for thirteen loaves. She only picked up two of the loaves and has to come back to bring my scarf. So she will be here a few times. You could make sure you see her then. At least that would be a start."

"It would. Crystal, you will tell me when she comes?"

"Of course I will."

And she did come, later that afternoon, with Crystal's scarf wrapped in white paper. Crystal called me as soon as Path walked through the door.

"Oh, Bird, come here. You must see this!"

Path unfolded the paper to reveal the headscarf and handed it to Crystal. And it was wonderful. It was a deep, dark red with a little blue, too, and golden stars all over it that looked like they were on fire. *You do not see colors this bright on cloth*, I thought. *This has come from someplace else.*

"The gift moves," said Path.

"It moves," said Crystal.

I looked at Path then, remembering that my father had told me to respect her and her way in the world. This piece of cloth was the sign and stuff of her way. And to make something so beautiful she must have gone deep indeed.

"Path," I said, "that is wonderful. It is beautiful. It—"

"Thank you," she said, turning to Crystal. "You can tie it up or pin it, and it is big enough to wear loose if you want."

Crystal was trying on the scarf, and her eyes shone with delight and amazement at having such a thing. Ma came over, and I could tell that she was impressed in spite of herself. She reached out, touched the cloth on Crystal's head, and looked at Path, saying, "It is beautiful. It makes my daughter more beautiful."

"Thank you," Path said again, and we were silent together for a moment, held by the beauty of the cloth and the passing of the gift among us all.

Crystal spoke. "Well. You must take some of your loaves, I think. What would you like?"

"What do you have now? I would take four with me today—that will be food for Heron and Aster and me."

Crystal began setting out bread. "This is a nut bread, and this is a crusty bread, and here is a loaf with cheese in it, and take this one, too." She held out an herb bread that we had made for the first time that morning. "This is fire-herb bread. We've never made it before, so you can tell us if you like it." Crystal wrapped up the loaves, and Path put them in her bag. "The gift moves," she said.

"It moves. I know I will like the fire-herb bread. Crystal, the scarf does look good on you."

"I thank you for it," my sister said, beaming.

As Path turned to go, I said, "Wait. Can I talk with you a minute?"

She stopped and waited for me. We walked out the door into the front garden together and stood by the gate.

139

"Path, can we meet sometime? To walk, to talk, to be friends?"

For a moment she looked frightened, like she might run away. But then she spoke, clutching her bread to her chest.

"Yes. Yes, we can."

"You know," I said, "tomorrow is a quarter day. We won't be baking."

Like most people, on the day of every quarter moon we did no work. The bakery would be closed, and I would have the whole day off. Maybe Path would be free, too.

"Usually we work on quarter days," said Path. "But tomorrow Heron will be gone, taking a load of cloth to the train. She said we could rest, that we'd have no more time to relax until Midsummer Day was over. So yes, I could come."

When I heard her words, I felt like flying. "I'll meet you on the beach in front of the Weavers' Yard an hour before noon," I said. "I'll bring some food. And some friends of mine if they can come."

"What will we do?" she asked.

"Something special. A surprise. You'll like it, I promise."

"All right, Bird. I'll meet you. An hour before noon." She turned and left in a hurry.

I watched her go, amazed at how much I wanted to be with her. I went back into the bakery to find Ma and Crystal looking over the headscarf.

"It's so bright, what color—"

"This will make your eyes stand out, Crystal. I've always said your eyes were the best part of your face. Wear this, and men will fall down over themselves to get in the door."

My sister had long wished for a serious boyfriend but hadn't found one yet, though she had hopes for Bright. As she and Ma talked, Walset, the cat, jumped on the counter, put his nose on the scarf, and sniffed. "Path," he said, "Path."

"I knew he liked her," Crystal said. "When she came in the other day, he marked her. How often does he do that for someone new? Hardly ever."

"That's true," Ma said, then to Walset, "Go now, get your claws away. We don't want any holes in this, do we?"

I began to think that my mother's opinion of Path was thawing a bit. After all, if the cat remembered her name, she was half family already.

We ate fish that night, with our bread and with fruit from Coral's next door. I told Ma about going to see Dad.

"And how was he?"

"You know, Ma, like he always is."

"Thinking too much, probably."

We passed more fish around.

"I talked to him about Path, Ma. How I'm worried about her."

"I don't know what there is to worry about for her," Ma said, "with what she can do with the cloth. Now you. You I am worried about."

She ate, silent, then went on. "You have big eyes for that girl. And you are right. There is a lot to see. A lot inside. But you be careful. There is much more there than you can see."

I looked at Crystal then, wondering if she too was thinking of Dad's words about the insects in the web. If Path was Spider-bit, then how? What was sleeping, dreaming in her? And what if it woke?

We finished dinner, and Crystal and I cleared the table. Fish for the cat, bread for the birds, bits of fruit for the raccoon who always came at night for scraps.

Across the fence at the Weavers' Yard, things were busy. Fires were going, light trees were up and shining—a real extravagance, but since it was all for Midsummer Day, an appropriate one. In the light I could see Path running to and fro, busier than I had ever seen her. I knew she would be tired when we met tomorrow.

I was up early, thinking of her. Walset was asleep at the foot of my bed and did not stir as I got up. Usually he would get up and demand food as soon as I woke. But not now. I saw the reason for this soon enough. A mouse's head lay on the floor next to the bed.

"So," I said to him, "you had a busy night, and now you're full of mouse."

He opened one eye and looked at me, then sighed and went back to sleep. I dressed silently and went downstairs. The bakery was quiet and clean. If this had been a regular day, we'd have been up and baking for half an hour already. I touched the counters, pans, and bowls. Everything was clean, waiting. And I felt like that, too, new and ready for something to happen. I picked up an orange and one of yesterday's rolls and walked to the beach.

The sun was just over the horizon, red in the haze. Already I could feel the heat. It would be hot today. There was not much wind, and the sea was almost calm, the surface smooth and unruffled. You don't often see it like this, and I took it as a sign. A clean day. A smooth day. I sat on the sand and ate, thinking about what we would do. I wanted to show Path something special, something she had never seen, and I decided to take her down the beach to the sea turtle nests. That would be something she had never seen. And it was my favorite thing on the beach, too. I finished eating and went back to the bakery.

Crystal was awake, making tea. She had set down a saucer of milk for Walset, who had decided he was hungry after all.

"Up already," said Crystal. "You're excited about your big day."

"Why do you say that?"

"Oh, Bird. I know you're going to see Path, find something to do with her."

"I just want to show her around. I thought I'd show her something she's never seen."

Crystal snorted with laughter. "I know what you want to show her, Bird."

I felt myself blush.

"And I'm right, too. Aren't I? I got you, Bird, I got you good." She laughed and gave me a cup of tea.

"No," I said, "I'm going to take her to the sea turtle nests. I thought I'd see if Rain and Rope would come, too. We'd bring food and eat and swim." I sipped my tea.

We heard the floor creak overhead and knew that Ma was waking up. On quarter days she would sleep late, and we always brought her breakfast in bed. Crystal set the kettle back on the stove for her tea.

"I'm going to find Rain and Rope and ask them to come," I said.

"Fine," said Crystal. "You'll be back here before you go?"

"Yes, I'll get some food together."

Crystal looked at me. "I know you really like Path. And I know she's the first girl you've felt drawn to like this. First is special. But remember, Bird, it's not always easy. To be together that way."

"What do you mean?" I asked.

"I mean," she paused, searching for words, "I mean that Path is wonderful. But I've thought about what you said yesterday."

"About what?"

"You said you were worried about her. And I think you're right to worry. I think she is very sad inside and very lonely. Very alone. Maybe more lonely than any person can fill. So be careful."

"I will. But I'm not worried about me. I'm worried about her."

"I know," said Crystal. "But I worry about you. That's what a sister is for, right? And," she added, "making you blush when I can."

"Right," I said.

I walked to Rope and Rain's house. They lived at a boat yard on the Sound, where they helped build all sorts of boats, some from plastic and some grown from seeds. Every so often, they would even build one from wood. I passed a row of four boats that had been planted a year ago. The hulls were bigger than me now, growing like giant squash with black leaves. In another year they'd be ready to finish, with sails and an electric motor, whatever the boat required. Ahead of me in their shed was a half-built wooden boat, planks curving up from its keel like the rib cage of a giant animal. Rain stood under it. She was my age but taller, with very short blond hair.

"Bird," she said, "what are you up to?"

"I thought I'd see if you and Rope want to come on a picnic with me and a friend. Someone I want you to meet."

"Who?" she asked.

"She's the new Hand at the Weavers'."

"I've heard about her. Never met her. The weavers never go out."

"I thought I'd take her to the sea turtle nests. And you and Rope can meet her. She doesn't know anybody yet. I'll bring the food."

"Sounds good to me. Rope," she shouted, "Bird's here."

Rope came running into the shed. He was Rain's twin but short and dark where his sister was tall and blond. He would leave the Banks soon after Midsummer Day to be a Hand on a Ship. I envied him this.

"Bird, how are you?" he said.

"Fine," I said. "I just asked Rain if the two of you could come with me for a picnic. And to meet someone. I'll bring the food."

"If you're bringing the food, I'd be a fool not to," he said.

"And the someone he wants you to meet is Heron's new Hand," said Rain.

"A weaver? You don't see much of them. She must be sneaking out. Heron doesn't let them go far, even on a quarter day," said Rope.

"Where's she from?" asked Rain.

"From the mountains in the west," I said. "From Boon."

"I'll look forward to meeting her," said Rope.

"Meet me on the beach in front of the Weavers' an hour before noon," I said.

"We'll be there," said Rain.

I ran back to the bakery to fix our food. We had plenty

of bread and rolls to choose from, and there was fruit and cheese as well. I thought about dried fish but decided it was a bad idea on a day as hot as this. I gathered up our lunch in a bag and added some bottles of water and a pie. Then I said goodbye to Crystal and went to find Path.

15

Path

Bird had said to meet him on the beach in front of the Weavers' Yard an hour before noon. Aster had warned me not to go.

"Path, if Heron finds out you've gone, she won't like it."

"So?" I asked. "I can have some time of my own. Heron's gone and we're not working today. So why not do what I want?"

"That's not how she sees it. If she finds out, she'll be mad, and you don't want her mad at you. I don't want her mad at you, either. She'll make it hard on everybody."

"She won't find out. And if I don't have to work, I don't see why I have to stay."

"She always finds out," said Aster. "You'll see."

* * *

Bird was waiting for me on the beach. "Path!" he called when he saw me. "I've brought us lunch. And we're going to meet some friends of mine. Go to a special place."

"What sort of place?"

"I want to surprise you. But it's my favorite place, almost. It's my favorite thing you can find on the beach."

"Then I'm sure I will be surprised," I said. We sat down on the sand to wait for his friends.

"What do you think of the Banks, now that you've been here a while?" he asked.

"I don't know. So far all I've seen is the Weavers' Yard, except for the bakery and the Circle and Sun Came's shop. Heron sent me there."

"You met Sun Came?"

"Yes."

"She's a Vulture, you know."

"I know. She showed me her robe."

"She did?"

"Yes. I didn't know what to say. I've met Vultures before, but only when someone died. And they didn't talk then."

"No, they never do. It was a gift from her, to show you who she is."

"I know."

Bird looked up and pointed. "There they are," he said. I saw a tall girl with short blond hair and a much shorter, heavyset boy with dark hair.

"I am Rain," said the girl, and "I am Rope," said the boy.

"Path Down the Mountain," I said.

"The gift moves," we said together. "It moves."

It turned out that Rain and Rope were twins. We set off south down the beach.

"How long have you been on the Banks?" asked Rope.

"Three weeks," I said.

"Hardly any time at all," said Rain. "Bird says you are Heron's new Hand."

"Yes. Midsummer Day will start my second Turn, and I'm here to weave."

"Rope is going to be a Hand, too," said Bird. "On a Ship."

"Really?" I asked. I had seen pictures of Ships but never thought I would see one or meet someone who would work on one.

"Yes," said Rope. "It's what I always wanted to do. My family builds boats, and I've always liked the ocean. I took every chance I had to meet Ship people when they came here. I got to know them and they liked me."

"And they asked him to be a Hand," finished Bird.

"When will you leave?" I asked.

"Right after Midsummer Day." Then Rope continued, "The Ship will stay offshore, and I'll go out on a boat to meet it. And there I'll be for Wheat, Sun, Turtle, Lizard, and Moon years."

"And I'll probably still be in the bakery," said Bird.

"It will be a good thing for the rest of us if you are," said Rain. "What did you bring to eat?"

"Bread, rolls, fruit, a little cheese," he said.

"Something sweet?"

"Something sweet, too," said Bird.

I remembered the tiny pies that Bird had made and the wonderful smell of the bakery. Whatever Bird had brought would be a welcome change from Heron's food.

"I think we're getting close," said Bird.

"Close to what?" I asked. I didn't see anything.

"There it is," Bird said.

I saw a small flag on a stick poking up from the sand. When we got closer, I could see a picture of Turtle on it.

"This is it," said Bird. "It's a sea turtle nest."

"Where?" I asked.

"Here. Underground," said Bird. "Under the flag is the place where a sea turtle laid her eggs. There are others, all along this stretch of beach."

"How many?"

"Probably twenty, twenty-five," he said. "Look, there's the next one." Bird pointed, and I could just make out another flag fluttering in the wind.

"What happens when they hatch?"

"They all hatch at once," Bird said, "and hundreds of

baby turtles dig their way out and run for the water as fast as they can. Seagulls, pelicans, and other birds come from everywhere to eat them."

"That's awful," I said, reaching for my Sun and Moon. "Do the birds eat a lot of them?"

"They eat as many as they can. But the little turtles are fast, too. And there are a lot of nests. In an hour's walk south you can see twenty more."

"How big are they?" I asked.

"When they hatch out," said Rope, "they're smaller than your hand. But when they grow up and come back to lay their eggs, they are bigger than you."

"Really?" I couldn't imagine a turtle that big.

"Yes," said Bird. "They live all their lives in the ocean, except when the females come to lay eggs in the late spring and summer. We only see them then. But now that we're here, I think we should eat."

Bird set down his bag and took out a bright blue cloth, which he spread on the sand. It was old, but I could see that it was Heron's work. He set out food and water and we ate in silence for a while, watching the waves. I kept imagining myself a tiny turtle, running from the birds on my way to the sea.

Finally Rope spoke. "Do you like being a Hand, Path?"

"It's hard. The work is hard. But I never thought of anything else."

"Me, too, I guess," he said. "I always knew I wanted to go to sea. But I wonder what it will be like, knowing I'll be with the same people on the same Ship for five years."

"And after that you'll stay on that Ship or find a new one," said Bird. "It's not like you're learning a trade you can take back here."

"No," said Rope. "Though maybe I could pilot a small boat around the Banks. But it wouldn't be the same."

"So when you leave to be a Hand, you won't be back. Not to live here, I mean," I said.

"No," said Rope.

Just like me, I thought. I knew I would not go back to Boon. I didn't know where I would go. Rope would have a Ship to take him. But I could see my life like a strip of cloth coming from the loom, one thread longer with each pass of the shuttle through the web. And no end to it but beauty and the cloth itself.

"What's wrong, Path?" asked Bird.

"Nothing."

"You looked all different. Lost all of a sudden."

"I was just thinking," I said.

"I think we ought to get in the water," said Rain. She stood up, pulled off her shirt, and stretched. Her tattoo was in the middle of her back. It was a bird's wing, bright red with the feathers outlined in black, big enough to fill her back from neck to waist.

Rope followed. On his chest and shoulders was a net with fish in it.

"And me," said Bird. There was a big dark bird on his chest, its yellow beak open and its wings curled around his heart.

"You've already seen part of mine," I said. Everybody sees the tattoo of footprints running around my right leg. I took off my tunic and stood, letting them see.

"It's my name," I said. They walked around me, following the footprints around my body, down to my foot.

"It's beautiful," said Bird. "I wondered where it went."

"Now you know," I said.

"Mine is my name, too," said Bird.

"And mine," said Rope. "But not Rain's."

"My wing is something I don't understand yet," she said. "And it's in a place I can't see. But I knew I had to have it just like it is."

We stood and looked at each other for a while. All our tattoos were new. You get one when you are near the end of your first cycle. Usually you dream it, and you visit Lizard with your parents and get your tattoo. Long ago, tattoos were made with ink, and the color was put into your skin with a needle. But now tattoos are alive, sort of. A virus lives in your skin, so they always stay bright and new. Sometimes they change color.

I wondered about Rain's wing. But I couldn't ask. She would tell me or show me if she wanted me to know. But even then I couldn't speak of it until she did. It was hers to give when she chose. Maybe someday I would tell Bird that the little pictures of trees and stones by the footprints on my body were landmarks on the trail down the South Fork of the New River to Boon. But not now. He could wonder. As I could wonder what his yellow-beaked bird was saying to his heart.

Bird broke the silence. "The gift moves," he said. We all replied.

Rain ran into the ocean and dived headfirst into the water, her red wing bright in the sun. "Maybe she can fly," I said.

"I don't know," said Bird. "Come on."

The water felt cool after the hot sun. The sea was the calmest I'd seen it since coming to the Banks. There was hardly any wind, and the surface of the water was almost smooth. No blowing spray or sand was getting in my eyes. I lay on my back, floating on the water. Bird stood next to me, looking at my tattoo.

"I'm not telling you," I said. "You'll have to wonder about it."

"Someday you will," he said.

"It will take more than a pie," I said. "More than a sack of pies."

"I'll think of something," he said.

I lay in the water and closed my eyes. It was the first peaceful time I had since before I left Boon. I knew it wouldn't last, and I was glad for it.

We swam until the sun was halfway to the trees, and then walked back up the beach. I was happy for the day and didn't even care if Heron found out where I'd been.

"Bird," I said, walking next to him. "You showed me something that is special to you. So it will be my turn next."

"When?" he asked, all eager.

"I don't know. I'll have to figure how to get away. Probably at night. I will leave you a message."

"Where will you leave it?" he asked.

"Where you will find it," I answered.

When we got to the beach in front of the Weavers' Yard, I said goodbye and walked to our tent. Heron was there. I could tell she was angry.

"So," she said. "You have been a busy girl."

"It's a quarter day. We weren't weaving. So my time was my own."

"Your own? Your own?" She stood over me. "As long as you are my Hand, nothing is your own. Nothing!" she shouted, and then she hit me in the ribs with her staff. The pain made me feel sick, and I fell to the floor.

"Now you will remember. Every hour, every minute, you are mine. I have a use for you, for everything you have and do. And I will give you much. I will give you a way with color and the cloth you will find nowhere else. And I will give you this"—she raised her staff—"when I have to. When you are weaving you are mine. When you are sleeping you are mine. And when you are out in the world you are mine most of all because then you are the weaver and maker of cloth, seen by all. You will have time for friends when you leave here and are no longer my Hand. And how much more will you be able to give them then, eh? After your time with me?"

My ribs hurt too much to speak. Heron seemed satisfied with my silence.

"Hard to talk? Yes, as it will be hard to weave, too, for the next day or two. You'll feel my staff every time you pull the beater. And you will remember."

She left. After a while Aster came in.

"I told you," she said. "She hurt you, didn't she?"

I nodded.

"She did it to me once. And I learned."

"What?"

"To give her what she wants. To be quiet and learn."

"No," I said.

"Path!" she said. "What are you going to do?"

"I don't know."

"She'll make you. She'll do what she has to. Just give it up and finish your time and leave."

"I don't know what I'll do. But not that."

16

Bird

I felt happier than I could remember. Crystal saw as soon as I came in the door.

"Well, Bird, it must have been a good day," she said.

"It was the best day. The best day I ever had."

"You went to the sea turtle nests like you said?" she asked.

"Yes. And we ate and swam."

"So you got to see her tattoo, huh?"

"I did."

"And where does it go?" Crystal asked.

"I'm not going to tell you. You'll have to wait and see." Midsummer Day wasn't far off, anyway. On Midsummer

Day everyone got to see everyone else's tattoos, when we threw our clothing in the fire.

"I'll be right next to you, then," she said. "Are you going to see her again?"

"She said she would let me know. She said she'd have to sneak out and leave me a message. So I'll wait and see."

That night I couldn't sleep. I thought of what we'd done all day, how Path looked when she ate the food I had made. I could tell she liked it, that it made her happy. I remembered her tattoo and how much I wanted to touch it. But she would have to ask me first. It was an unusual tattoo. It's not uncommon to have a tattoo that tells your name. Mine is like that. But Path's was large and elaborate. Next to the line of footprints winding around her body were little pictures—rocks, trees, buildings, a river, even some sheep. I wondered if it was a map.

And she had said we'd meet again. Finally I fell asleep, wondering where she might leave her message to me.

But there was no message the next day, and none the day after that or the day after that. I looked everywhere I could think of and checked the place where I'd left the birdman by the fence a couple of times each day. But there was nothing, and I began to worry. I worried that Path had changed her mind, that she didn't want to see me. I worried that she had been kidding me all along. I worried that Heron had found out where she'd gone and wouldn't let her leave.

I took every chance I could to look into the Weavers' Yard and caught occasional glimpses of Path outdoors, always busy with cloth. I could never catch her eye.

After a week Ma talked to me. "I'm concerned about you, Bird," she said. "You have your head full of that girl at the Weavers'—Path."

"I just want to see her again, sometime."

"Sometime. And in the meantime you're sad and droopy. Slow in your work, too."

"No, I'm not," I said. "Look at this." I pointed to what I'd been doing—the thirteen pans, with thirteen muffins in each one I'd just pulled out of the big oven. "I think I'm doing well."

"Maybe you are," said Ma. "But you're not happy about it. Get out and do something with your friends instead of looking over at the Weavers' all the time. If she wants to see you, she will."

I waited three more days, and then Path's message came. I found it by the fence where I'd left the birdman. It was a tightly rolled piece of blue cloth lying on the scrubby grass. I picked it up and took it inside with me, afraid Heron would see me. When I was alone, I unrolled the little cloth. She had written on it in fabric paint. "Meet me on the beach in front of the bakery at midnight," it said.

So I would see her again. And find out what was happening to her, why her life was so hard.

I stayed awake long after Ma and Crystal had gone to

sleep, long after the lights had gone off in the Weavers' Yard. When it was time, I quietly opened the bakery door and slipped out into the night. I walked to the beach and sat on the sand. In a few minutes she was there. She sat down beside me. I could just make out her shape, and my memory filled in the details: her brown skin, her small mouth, her bright eyes that could look right through you. Until that moment I didn't know she was so alive in my mind. I felt watery inside and wanted to touch her so much that it ached. But I was afraid to, afraid she'd run away if I did.

"Bird," she said.

"Path. You're here." I let go the weight of worry I'd been carrying.

"Yes. I'm sorry it has been so long."

"What happened?" I asked. "I was worried when I didn't hear from you."

"When I got back to the Weavers' Yard, Heron was there. In our tent. She knew where I'd been and was very angry."

"What did she do?" I asked.

"She told me that as long as I was her Hand, I was hers. She said I would have time for friends after that, when my time as Hand was over. And then . . ."

"And then what?" I asked.

"And then she hit me with her staff. Here." She lifted her tunic and pointed to her side. There was a big bruise there, against her ribs. It was still purple. "It hurt a lot. And she said the pain would help me remember."

"No! And then what happened?"

"I just did my work and waited," she said. "I wanted to see you, and I knew I could sneak out again if I waited long enough."

"What will she do if she finds out?" I asked.

"I don't know. I think I can keep her from finding out."

"How?"

"I am good at that," she said. "Look. When you took me to the turtle nests, you showed me something special to you from your home. And I want to show you something special from my home. Only I can't show you the place. But I can show you what I learned there. And that will be a return of the gift to you. Would you like that?"

"Yes, I would," I answered.

"Then follow me," she said and led me down the beach until we were past the Weavers' Yard. She turned away from the beach and walked inland to the road. We kept going south, to the place where the road turns into a path with trees on both sides. *Where on earth is she going,* I wondered. And then she stopped and turned to me on the moonlit path.

"You gave me much last time we were together, Bird. And what I have for you in return is a kiss."

My heart leaped at this, but she went on.

"A kiss freely given, yours for the taking, as soon as you can get close enough to touch me."

And then she was gone, just like that. Vanished into the

trees beside the path. I thought I heard movement to my left, toward the beach, so I dashed that way. I kept quiet, knowing that calling her name would do no good. I stood under a small pine tree and heard a sound above me, and there she was, standing two branches above my head.

"Oh, Bird, I think I'm too far away to touch. But I'll come closer." And with that she jumped to the ground right behind me and was off before I could move. *This is what I have given my heart to*, I thought.

I followed the way she had gone, caught sight of her ahead in the moonlight, and ran as fast as I could. I thought I was getting closer, and breathing hard, I put all my strength into my legs when I saw her ahead of me. I should have been looking at the ground because I tripped over an old root of a pine tree and fell, which knocked the wind out of me.

"Almost," she said, standing over me. "Almost close enough." And she was gone again.

I got up and followed. She was headed to the beach, running over the dunes. I came up over the top of a dune to find the shore empty. At the edge of the surf were her clothes in a neat pile. I stood by them and looked out over the waves for a sign of her, a splash from a head or arm against the sea and breaking waves. Nothing. I started to walk into the surf, ready to swim, when I felt a touch on the back of my neck. I turned around, all goosebumps.

"Close enough," she said and kissed me very softly. "The gift moves." She put her clothes on, and we sat on the sand. I was still out of breath and sore from my fall.

"It moves," I said.

"I never did go in the water. I was hiding just over the dune. I figured you wouldn't notice me running once you saw my clothes on the sand."

She was right. The night was quiet and calm, with almost no wind. The moon was shining on the water, and I could see ghost crabs darting in and out of the surf. We sat there, side by side, where the highest waves would just touch our toes. The tide was coming in.

"You were ready to go in, weren't you?" she said with a laugh.

"I was. I was. You ran so fast, climbed so fast. Where do you get this?"

"I get the muscles from weaving."

"From weaving?" I asked.

"Yes. You have to use every muscle in your body to work a loom. Your shoulders, arms, waist, hips, legs, and feet. Everything moves in rhythm. And you don't stop. We weave eight to ten hours a day, and it makes you strong."

"I didn't know it was like that. I thought it was kind of quiet and calm," I said.

"And the cloth comes out of the loom all by itself? Just like the bread and cakes and rolls come out of the oven by themselves?"

I thought of our long days in the bakery. "No, I guess not."

"My people taught me to move and hide. It comes from growing up with the sheep. That is what I wanted to show you from my home, in return for taking me to the turtle nests. It's something I learned there."

"How?"

"Everything you do with the sheep, everything outside, the herding, the feeding, looking for the lost sheep, we made games of it. Herding sheep might turn into a race, to see who could get to the pasture first to gather the flock. And we'd play a game called you-can't-touch-me in order to learn the land. I was playing that with you, only you didn't know we were playing it."

"How did it work?"

"One of us would hide and the others would try to find him. Or her. That way you had to learn the land, up, down, inside and out, whether you were hiding or looking. They never found me, but I always found them."

"They never found you?"

"Never. Part of the fun is to hide so close that you can see and hear the people who are looking for you."

"You must have been good at it."

"I had to be. They made fun of me because of my mother. Because she was from the city and a dancer. They thought she felt she and her girl were too good for them."

"That's cruel," I said. "And when she was gone, what happened then?"

165

"Then it was worse. Because all the adults felt sorry for me and tried to make me happy. Which only made the rest of the children jealous. But I showed them I was better." She pulled herself up, proud. "I could move faster than any of them. Faster and farther. And leap and climb. I remember sitting high up in a tree watching my cousins Sparrow and Owl underneath, trying to find me. I could have peed on their heads. I probably should have. That's the kind of thing they would remember."

This still hurts you, I thought. "I'm glad you didn't pee on mine."

She laughed. "It sounds like a game," she said. "And it was. But it was life and work, too. I had to prove myself to them all the time. Over and over. I even did things that were foolish and dangerous, things that might have got me hurt."

Again I remembered the dye running down her arms. "But you didn't get hurt?"

"No, but my cousin Owl did. I jumped across a ravine and dared him to follow me. He tried and fell and broke his ankle. After that my father kept me close."

"What was that like?"

"The kids were jealous of me for being with him all the time. He was the leader of the whole family, and I had him to myself. But he was trying to take care of me. He knew I missed my mother. He would tell me, 'You want to find your mother, look to your feet. You are sure-footed as a cat,

166

same as her.' So I used my feet, showed the others what my feet could do. And I think I scared him a little."

"How so?"

"I might have been sure-footed as a cat, but the other kids weren't. Not Owl, that's for sure. I was a risk not just to myself but to others, and so he culled me from the herd. But that had a good side, too. Because he took me to the weavers."

"Where you found your mother in a different way?"

"Yes. But there's something else. I've never told this to anyone. It's like the one thing I have. The thing I hold back. I don't tell it because I'm afraid of what will happen if I say the words." She held out her Sun and Moon pendant. "But I will tell you. If I can. I will tell you how I got this."

17

Path

Bird watched me, expectant, waiting for me to speak. The lump in my throat was huge, too big to speak around.

"Path," he said.

I waited, listened to the sea wash back and forth, looked at the moon low on the horizon. Then I swallowed and spoke.

"How I got this." I took off my necklace, held the Sun and Moon pendant, turning it over and over in my hands. Sun, Moon, Sun, Moon. "I didn't tell you the truth before, not all of it. My mother was never happy in Boon. Never very happy with my father. I guess maybe she was at first, but after a while what was there for her? Me and the sheep. No place to dance, no city, no friends. Just a cold tent and Ram, my father, who thought of the whole family as his herd, with him the lead ram. My mother used to talk to me about the life she had left behind, how wonderful it was. Tall buildings, lights, music and dancing and plays all the time. So when she couldn't stand it anymore, she left. She took me with her, got on the bus, and went back to Rollydee."

"It must have been a big change," said Bird.

"It was. It was as wonderful as she had said it was. My mother's parents were actors. Silk, her mother, and Far Talking, her father. When we went to Rollydee, we moved in with them. And it was great. There were all sorts of people—artists, musicians, actors. It was the first time I ever saw a piece of Heron's cloth. One of my mother's dresses was made from it. Everybody came to see my mother and her parents. And Silk and Far Talking were glad to have her back and me with her. Her old life started again. She began to dance with her parents, and she was happy. And we had to travel. They would put on plays as far away as Lanta, and when it was time to go we would all go together."

I looked at Bird, who was watching me, intent on my story. The water had risen to where we were sitting, so we moved up the beach a little bit.

"I enjoyed that. I would get passed from hand to hand backstage while my mother was dancing, and I got a lot of attention from everybody. But one day it changed."

"How?"

"I was watching my mother dance from the wings, backstage. It was something fast, I can't remember what. There were a lot of leaps in it, and the drums were playing, and the music was getting louder. She leaped high into the air, higher than I'd ever seen her. And I called to her, 'Mama!' Just because it was so good, what she was doing. And she heard me, looked my way for an instant. Then she lost her focus and fell."

I couldn't talk for a while after that. I had to get up and walk. I had never talked about this. I thought I had left it behind for good. But there I was. Meanwhile, Bird was sitting still, watching me walk. I think if he'd got up and come to me, I'd have run. But he didn't. After a while, I sat by him again.

"She was all right. She got up and finished the dance. But after that she wouldn't dance with me watching her, not onstage. Not in a performance. From then on, when she went on a trip, she would leave me behind in Rollydee. I felt like I was dragging her down. I felt like a weight on her. At first she would leave me at Children's House with all the other kids. But I didn't like it there, and I wanted my mother. I was used to being with my family in Boon and hated being with children I didn't know. I was fast and small and knew how to run. So I did. I would go back to Silk and Far Talking's place and look for someone I knew to take care of me. There were always actors and musicians going in and out, and somebody would take me in. Then when my mother got back, she would be upset. Mad at me, mad at Children's House. Finally she gave up and arranged for me to stay with friends while she was gone. But her friends had lives, too. They were artists, musicians, other theater people. They were busy. Too busy for a little girl who was crying for her mother. It couldn't last.

"I remember the night they talked about it. They sat at the table in the big room at their studio. It was living room, dance studio, and rehearsal space all in one. There were mirrors on one wall and a wooden floor. I was playing in the next room where they kept all the costumes. I would try on one thing, then another. I heard them talking around the corner, through the door. And I realized they were talking about me.

"'Cat, you can't do this to her. She is your child. Your flesh. Ours, too. She needs you, your hand, your time,' said Silk.

"'I have to dance,' said my mother. 'I found that out while I was in Boon with all those sheep. I won't give it up.'

"'You don't have to give it up,' said Far Talking. 'Just be her mother, too.'

"'Be a mother, too. When I am a mother, that is all I am. She is all I know. What she needs, what she wants, where she is. I can feel her in the room better than I can feel my own feet. I can feel her call to me. And I fall. If she would stay at Children's House, maybe this would work. But we've tried it. You know it doesn't work. So.'

" 'So what?' asked Silk.

" 'So I will take her back to her father. You know she's not happy here. She will like it better with the people she came from. She can run wild in the hills with the rest of them.'

"And I heard it all, there in the next room. She was going to take me back to Boon. Oh, Bird, I don't know. I don't know if I can tell you this. I promised myself I would never tell, never say it. This is what scares me."

"But I'd like to hear it. I hope you can tell me."

"I'll try," I said and waited a while until I had calmed down. Then I took a deep breath and went on.

"She took me back on Midsummer Day. We got off the bus at Boon and started up the path to the Circle. My mother was moving very slowly, holding my hand. I asked her what we were doing.

" 'Hush, Path. Everything in its time.'

"Only when she saw the smoke from the fire rise over the trees did she pick up the pace a little bit. By the time we got to the Circle, the festival was almost over. Everyone was standing around the fire, throwing in their gift. My mother started to dance then, a slow, side-to-side step. She kept hold of my hand. So I danced with her as best I could.

I told myself maybe she wanted to show off how pretty I was, how I had grown. I didn't really believe she would leave me there.

"She danced right up to the fire and put down my hand. It was very hot. She was wearing her wool tunic, the one she had worn the day we had left Boon. She took it off and flung it over her head into the fire. By this time every eye in the Circle was on us. She held my hand and looked around until she saw my father, Ram. And she danced us around the fire to where he was. And then we . . ."

And now I had got to the part of the story I had never told anyone. This far the telling had taken me. It was a long thread, pulling words up from inside me, pulling the warp through the loom of my own life. Only now the telling was pulling up the hard things, hidden things. Instead of knots to ease through heddles and reed, I felt rocks and ice deep in my belly. I didn't know how to change them into words and get them through my mouth, didn't know what would happen if I did.

"Bird, I really don't know if I can tell you this," I said, getting up again to run down the beach, feet in the surf, splashing, testing Bird to see if he would follow. But he didn't. I waited, wanting to be sure he wouldn't move. But he was still. So I went back to where he was sitting.

"And then—this is the hard part." I swallowed and went on, feeling words pushing at the back of my throat, rocks and ice no longer. Sun Came was right. They wanted out.

"She took my hand and put it in my father's hand. She gave me back to him.

"'The gift moves,' she said."

Now my words began to come faster and faster, the thread of telling slipping through my hands all at once. "He replied with the usual 'It moves.' And then she turned to dance away. Her favorite dance. The Cat Dance from 'The Story of Sun and Moon's Daughter.' The dance she used to do carrying me in her arms, her little kitten. When she began to dance I knew she was really going to leave me. She turned, and I reached out to hold on to her and grabbed this." I took off my necklace and held out the Sun and Moon pendant. "It came away in my hand. It was on a beaded necklace, and the beads flew everywhere, falling stars in the firelight.

"Then she was gone. It was as if she was flying, like a bird. As if she had turned loose of something that had been weighing her down for years. That something was me. I called out to her, screaming to make her turn around and see me, to take me back. I tried to go to her, but my father held me tight. When I realized she wasn't going to come back, wasn't even going to turn around and look at me again, I bit my father's hand to make him let go of me so I could jump in the fire. I wanted the flames, the bright heat. If my mother didn't want me, I wanted to die. But my father was too strong. He just held me and wouldn't let me move."

"That's awful."

"She danced out of the firelight, out of the Circle, and out of Boon. I never saw her again. This is what I have of her now." I put the necklace back over my head. "I have never been back to the fire since. Each year, when Midsummer Day came, I hid high up the mountain. They knew they couldn't find me."

"And that's all you have left?" Bird asked, pointing to my Sun and Moon. "You've never heard anything about her, no stories, nothing?"

"Nothing," I said. "I might as well have been dead to her." I waited, feeling the last pebble of the telling rise up in my throat. My one little hope. I would tell it all.

"But sometimes I thought that if I could learn enough, if I was good enough, that she would somehow hear about this weaver who made wonderful cloth. And she would try to find that weaver. Finally she would find her and it would be me, and then she would see me for who I really was, someone she would want. And she would love me. And I would be home. But I will never be good enough. Never. It doesn't matter." The weight of my words hit me, the weight of telling what I had promised myself I would never tell. And I was lost. I felt a rush inside me, something let go, and I must have screamed there on the beach.

Bird called. "Path, Path! Are you all right?"

I didn't answer. So this is what I got for telling the truth I had kept inside. I started to pound the sand with my fists, one after the other, over and over. I saw that Bird was scared. *I am too,* I thought, *I am too.* Finally I got tired of pounding and stopped. Bird came to me then, touching my shoulder. I didn't want to be touched, not by him, not by anyone. I didn't want any more good things that would only be taken away.

"No," I said. "No. Not now. Not ever." And I ran, as fast as I have ever run, along the surf to the south, away from Heron's, the bakery, away from him, too. I wanted to make my body carry me as far as it could, and then I would hide. I heard Bird calling for me, and all I could think of was hiding. I stayed under a pine tree until almost dawn. Then I went back up the beach to Heron's. The old woman was awake, but if she saw me come in, she gave no sign.

18

Bird

"No," she said. "No. Not now. Not ever." And then she ran away fast, faster than I ever could. I tried to follow but knew I had lost her after a few strides. Still I followed, running south down the beach, hoping to see her, hoping she would stop, change her mind, turn around.

When I was winded and could run no more, I stopped. I waded into the surf to cool off and get my breath back, then walked back over the dunes to the path, calling her name as I headed north. But there was no sign of her. No track, no broken branch. Nothing. She was gone as if she had never been there at all. It was as if she had made sure she was faster than me, made sure she could get away from me, before she would give me anything precious. Like her kiss.

And it was that way with her story, too. She was testing me, I knew. Getting up to see if I would follow. Something had told me not to do that, to stay put. And I guessed that was right. Because she had come back, she had told her story, let out what she had kept in. It cost her, it hurt her to do it, I knew. When she was pounding the sand with her fists, it was as if she were fighting the immovable thing, hitting the thing she couldn't change. She could outrun me but not what was inside her. Maybe she would feel lightened by telling me this at last, maybe would see she could go on.

By now the path had widened into the street, and I walked in the dark past Coral's, past the gate of the Weavers' Yard. I waited there for a long time, hoping that Path might come back, though in my heart I knew better. She would not let me see her until she was ready. I knew her well enough now to be sure of that. It made me feel lonely. I missed her, felt her absence deep inside me. It was the same ache I had felt when she sat beside me on the sand and I wanted to touch her. Only worse now.

"Path. Please come back. Don't stay away," I said, talking to the night as if it had ears and a voice of its own to answer back. But my words flew away like moths in the night, and all I heard in reply was the slow breath of the ocean, the breaking waves. Then I left the gate and went back to the bakery, careful not to wake anybody up. I didn't want Ma to know how late I'd been out.

Every night sound woke me up. I was afraid for Path and had bad dreams of cloth, looms, and dye, all menacing and dangerous.

The morning found me just as tired as the night before. We had to do the work of an ordinary day, filling the hungry people who came in, plus making even more bread and cakes, pies, pastries, and everything else for the feast and the fire.

I worked without stopping, all day and into the night. There was no time for a meal, just time to grab up a piece of what I was making and eat it hot from the oven like fire in my mouth. I wondered if that's how Path's story felt to her, the words and the telling hot coals on her tongue. I wished I could talk to my sister, to tell her what Path had said, what had happened. But there was no time.

All day long I couldn't keep Path out of my head. I remembered her kiss, so soft and warm. She had come up behind me like a ghost, and when she stood naked next to me I was afraid to touch her, afraid she'd vanish. Of course, given how easily she'd outrun me, she would have vanished. More than once Ma had to remind me to get back to work.

"Bird. We are never going to get through half of what we have to do if you don't move, if you don't work."

She would give me her knowing look, and I wondered

if she had been waiting up for me the night before. Each time, I would get to work again, Path not far from my mind. I couldn't imagine being rejected by my mother that way. Ma and Dad had never spent much time living together, but they were very close, and they always cared about Crystal and me, always took care of us, sometimes too much care maybe. But I had not thought about the alternative until now. Until Path told me her story. Today the bakery didn't really seem so bad.

I tried to put myself in her place, to subtract everything familiar from my life: the bakery, Ma, Crystal, Dad, the town, and all my friends. And I couldn't. I couldn't imagine life without them, couldn't imagine me without them. No wonder Path held on to her Sun and Moon for dear life, no wonder she held on to her mother's story. It was all she had. Except she had given the story to me.

I looked down at the tray of loaves I had just taken out of the oven. I mean I *really* looked at it, like Path would look at cloth. I saw the hard brown crust of each loaf, the tiny bubbles where moisture had baked out in the oven, smelled the aroma of the bread. Ma and Crystal and I had made these, and we were part of them. And not just us. The town and everybody else were all in there too. I was holding all the things Path had given up or lost in her life. Her story was in my hands.

I thought of Path at the loom, making cloth for the sake of beauty and nothing else. And then I knew how alone she was and what a gift her story had been to me. I wanted to return the gift with what I had. I wanted her to have a home.

Surely I would be able to see her at Midsummer Day. She would be with Heron at the weavers' tent. It was the busiest place there, with cloth and banners and all sorts of stuff for the taking.

I could introduce her to more of my friends. That would be a start. Crystal could take her to the Girls' House. She could make friends there, too. And she could meet Dad.

That was how the day passed for me. Work on the outside, and on the inside thoughts about Path that bounced back and forth from fear to hope and back again. Finally, long into the night, we shut down the ovens and got ready for bed.

"Bird," Ma said, "You want to have fun, run, dance, see your weaver friend, then you wait two more days. On Midsummer Day you can have all you want of that. But not now. We three have too much to do."

"I know, Ma. I'll rest. Don't worry."

"Worry? Why should I worry?" And with that she left.

19

Path

Aster woke when I came into the tent. "Where have you been?" she asked.

"Out. On the beach, walking."

"Walking all night? You look awful."

"I look fine," I said. I had done too much talking about myself that night, and now Aster would not let me be quiet.

"Let me get you some food, Path. You must be tired."

"No!" I said. "I don't want anything. Just leave me alone." I turned my back on her and changed my clothes, putting on my dye gear. I didn't want help. I didn't want hands offering me things. Not Bird's hands, not Aster's. I would take care of myself. I picked up a banana and left the tent, heading for the ocean. I sat down on the sand and watched the sun come up while I ate.

Why had I told all of that to Bird? He did that to me, made me let out more than I meant to. Starting with my name in return for his pies. The telling made it grow, get big, fill me up. "Mama," I said, holding the Sun and Moon pendant. "Mama." I felt the word on my tongue, felt it leave my lips. And the wind from the sea took it as quickly as I said it. "Mama," I said a third time. And the wind took that, too. I had not said that word in a long time. Maybe not since she had left me at the fire. The word that made her fall. The word that made her leave me. The word that would not turn her head when my father held me by the fire. Yet I could say the word again and again, as if it came out of a deep pit inside me where there was no bottom. I could call my mother over and over, and no amount of words would make things unhappen.

Mama. A word of power. But not the power to take me home. Not the power to take me anyplace else. Here I was, Heron's Hand, and here I would stay. I finished my banana and went back to the tent. Aster and I walked to the loom-house to start the day's work. She was quiet now. I hoped she would stay that way.

Heron was waiting for us. "A late night you had, girl."

"So?"

"So I can't have tired hands on the cloth. Not now. We dye today and tomorrow. You know that."

"I know. I'm not tired. And my hands are steady. See?" I held both hands out in front of me for Heron to see.

"Hmm. You have steady hands. But tired eyes. Big circles." She hit the floor with her staff. "Big circles." She walked all around the room as she talked. "I know where you go, girl. You go to see that boy from the bakery."

I stiffened at her words.

"Yes," she said, "I pay attention to what you do. Because you are mine. My Hand while you are here." She put her right hand in front of my face, in front of her eyes, flexed one finger after the other. "And I expect you to be ready. To be at your best. Now you have that boy on your mind. How can you learn, how can you work, if your mind is somewhere else?"

"My mind is right here," I said.

"You see that it stays here. And you stay here with it. You are mine, girl. You are mine. You will learn this lesson." She left the loomhouse, and we knew to follow. Aster looked at me. "See," she said, speaking quietly so Heron wouldn't hear, "she doesn't want us going out. Having friends. You don't want to make her mad."

"I've already done that. She's already hit me. What else could she do?"

"She hit me once," said Aster. "When I dropped a load of wet cloth in the sand. Not as hard as she hit you. It was the look on her face that I remember. She was cold, not angry. Like I was a thing to her then. Later she was different, and I was a person again. But for that moment, when she hit me, I was a thing. I don't forget that."

Up ahead of us Heron was lighting the methane burner under the big dye vat. It made a loud whump when it caught, and then I saw the blue flame flecked with yellow, which would heat the dye. We knew what to do. Aster and I climbed the steps to the platform that circled the vat. We undid the latches holding the cover down and rolled it up. It was made of a special fabric, canvas covered with some sort of plastic. It kept the heat in and the rain out. With the cover, the dye would stay hot overnight and take less time to bring to working temperature the next day.

"Come, you two," Heron called from below. "We've a lot of cloth to move."

Back to the loomhouse we went, past the now-empty drying racks we would soon fill. Stacked in the back of the loomhouse was the last of our cloth for Midsummer Day, eight hundred square feet of undyed cloth, in five strips that were twenty feet long and eight feet wide. This would cover our stall in the Circle, the same color as the cloth we had made for the fire pavilion. We would dye half of it today and half tomorrow. And we would be finished with work until Midsummer Day. Aster and I each picked up one end of a bolt of cloth, lifted it to our shoulders, and took it to the dye vat.

"This is more than we made last year," she said as we climbed up to the platform.

"How much did you make then?"

"Maybe half this much for the stall." We set the cloth down on the platform. The gas burner roared beneath us. We could feel the heat rise up through our feet.

"This year is the first time she's made a cloth covering for the weavers' stall in the Circle. Before, she always used the cloth to drape over the front, but this is new. We'll have to stitch it all together once we get it there."

We walked back to the loomhouse, picked up each of the remaining four bolts of cloth we would dye, and took them one by one to the vat. Heron went with us as we took the last load of cloth. Her anger was gone, and she was her usual self, intent on the cloth and showing us what to do.

Soon the rhythm of the work took hold of us. The cloth went into the vat in long strips, and we worked it into the hot liquid quickly, stirring with long wooden paddles. This was still new to me, and I watched Heron and Aster and did what they did. At times like this I could fall into the work, drawn by something deep in the cloth and color. It was like the ocean. I had not been there long but already the sound of the waves was a part of me. I could feel the pull, in and out, in and out, and put myself into the work in the same way. I could forget myself and become hands on the cloth. Nothing more.

* * *

But the sound of the fire roused me, called me back. We were almost done with the batch of cloth. Heron had put the sodium sulfite in to fix the dye, and we had turned up the burner to get the liquid almost to a boil. The fire. It burned hot beneath us, hungry for air. I knew I couldn't avoid it, not this time. I had never been back to the fire on Midsummer Day since my mother had left me. But this year I knew I would go. Heron would make me. She would close every exit there was.

It was full dark by the time we finished work. We shut down the burner, covered the vat, and went back to our tents. Aster and I ate in silence, sharing the last of the bread Crystal had given me. When I was sure Heron was asleep, I walked to the gate and looked down the street to the bakery. Quiet now. They were all asleep in there, Bird and Crystal and their ma. I wished I could have what they had. But it was not for me. My mother had shown me that.

"Path." A small voice from the pavement. I looked down. It was Walset, their cat. I picked him up and held him, purring fur. He was like the sheep. Simple, warm. He said my name over and over. I scratched him under his chin and set him down. "Go now, cat," I whispered. I didn't want to wake Heron. He walked away, tail high, and jumped over the fence into the yard of the bakery.

* * *

When we met at the loomhouse in the morning, Heron told Aster to take a load of cloth to the Circle for our stall. "Let the carpenters cut wood to fit the cloth and not the other way around," she said.

Aster and I loaded the cloth onto our big cart. "She's lying," I said.

"Heron?" she asked. "About what?"

"About the stall. It's already built. When I took the Sun and Moon robes, I met the carpenter who was to build it, and he said it was his next thing to do. So there's no need to take a load of cloth for the carpenters to measure. They're already done," I said.

"Then she wants me gone. So she can be alone with you," said Aster.

"Yes."

"You'd better be careful. Just give her what she wants. Wait a while, and when Midsummer Day is past she'll get looser. You have to get along. She'll make you, Path."

"No," I said.

Aster left, pushing the heavy cart. She would be gone for hours, and I would be alone with Heron.

20

Bird

When I was sure Ma was asleep, I tiptoed out of my bedroom and tapped on Crystal's door.

"Bird?" she whispered.

"Yes."

"Are you all right? I could tell you weren't yourself today. You kept doing things wrong."

"I know."

"You even forgot to put the yeast in a batch of rolls. It's a good thing I caught it, or Ma would have been mad."

"I did that? I'm sorry, Crystal. I didn't mean to."

"I know. But Ma is pretty upset. She's not going to show it now because there's so much to do. But she will later."

"Why? What does she say?"

"She stayed up last night until you came in. She kept me up, too, walking around, picking things up, putting them down. She was in a state, I'll tell you."

"Did you talk to her?"

"Yes. I got up and asked her to go to sleep. And she said she wouldn't, not with you out there doing who knows what with that weaver girl. She said Path was going to be trouble for you. Not trouble because she was bad or mean. Trouble because she had trouble of her own."

"Then she's right." I told Crystal what Path had told me, as quickly as I could. Then I asked if she could introduce Path to some of her friends from the Girls' House.

"Of course I will, Bird."

"And you know how beautiful your headscarf is. I bet the other girls would want to know someone who could make things like that."

"They would, that's true," she said. "But look. It's late and getting later and I don't know how we're going to get through tomorrow. Let's sleep now. We'll both see Path on Midsummer Day."

"Yeah. You're right. See you in the morning."

"Good night."

I left Crystal and went back to my own bed as quietly as I could so as not to wake Ma. I lay there for a long time, unable to sleep. I thought about Path and feared for her. I wondered what was happening to me that had made her so important. She had changed me somehow, just in the few days I had known her. Now I knew that the simple world of the town and Ma and Dad and Crystal and the bakery was not something I could count on, even if I was counting on it for something to complain about.

Finally I did fall asleep, only to be woken up in the middle of the night by Walset touching my cheek with his paw.

"Go away," I said.

"Path," he said, "Path." He said her name over and over, until I quieted him down by putting him under the covers. I wondered what had put Path in the cat's mind. I wondered if she was all right.

It was still dark when Ma woke us. "Up, you, Bird, Crystal. Too much to do, too little time."

I rolled over in the bed and there was Walset, wrapped around my legs. I remembered him coming to my bed, saying Path's name. So it wasn't a dream. I sat up on the edge of the bed, scratched myself, and stood up. Walset stretched and lay down again, kneading my pillow with his paws and saying his mother's name over and over. "Twelve," he purred. "Twelve."

"So you're a kitten again," I said. He looked at me with one eye. "Why did you talk about Path in the night? Tell me that, cat." But he was intent on the pillow and his inner world.

Downstairs Ma was measuring flour, Crystal lighting

ovens. I picked up a stale bun from the day before and ate it. We were making ring loaves, a kind of bread we made only for Midsummer Day. Big loaves with a hard shiny crust. We would braid dark and light dough together and bake the bread in a circular pan shaped like a big O so the bread would be a circle, like the circle of Years.

I went to the storeroom and brought out the circular pans, all fifty of them, which we used only once a year. I washed them while Crystal and Ma got the dough ready. These loaves would take three bakings, since we would make one hundred fifty of them. Enough for everybody in town to have at least a bite, with more left to go into the fire at the end. Then I heard the front door bell ring. Someone had come in.

"Bird," said Ma. "Go see what they want. Quick, now."

I dried my hands. People get hungry all the time, and the hard thing about the days before Midsummer Day was that people still came in for bread. So we would run back and forth between the kitchen and the front room all day. I went into the front room, and there was Heron's other Hand. A tall girl in a blue weaver's shift, dark hair in a knot on top of her head. Blue eyes, freckled arms. She looked around like a squirrel, nervous. What was her name? I couldn't remember.

"I am Bird Speaks," I said, "and you are . . ."

"Aster. I am Aster. From the Weavers'." Her eyes darted

around the room, out the window to Heron's place. "I shouldn't be here," she said.

"Do you want some bread?"

"No. Yes. Then if Heron sees that I have been here, I can tell her I was hungry. But I have come because of Path."

"Path." I felt cold inside, afraid for her. "Is she all right?"

"Yes. But I am worried about her. The night before last she was out all night. And I think she was with you. She came back and wouldn't talk. She is so upset, so tired," said Aster. "I'm worried that she will make a mistake because she is tired and ruin some of the cloth."

"And if that happened?"

"Then Heron would be mad at her. I don't know what she'd do."

"I know she hit Path. She showed me," I said.

"Then you know what Heron can do," said Aster. "But that's not all. I worry that Path might make a mistake that would hurt herself, and not just the cloth. We work with so many dangerous things. The dyes are poison. And there is acid, and everything is boiling hot sometimes. And there is the fire, too."

"But what can I do?"

"I don't know. Remember that she needs to rest. Remember that Heron doesn't want her to have anything to do with you. She'll get in trouble if Heron finds out."

I didn't want that, I knew.

"I have to go," she said. "Heron sent me to the Circle with this load of cloth. I have to get there and back fast."

"Take this bread, then." I handed her a couple of loaves. "The gift moves."

"It moves," she said and left, pushing her big cart down the street. I turned back to the kitchen door and saw Ma glaring at me through the window.

"You're getting awfully popular with the weavers," she said.

"Ma—"

"They seldom come here. Seldom. Heron once a month and the Hands once or twice a year. And now. First Path and now this one."

"She just wanted some bread, Ma. That's all."

"Bread. And talk. Talk about that Path. She is trouble for herself and trouble for you."

Ma went back to the big table, helping Crystal knead the white dough. "Bird," she called. "You punch down that dark dough, now. Maybe we'll get this done before sundown." From then on, when the bell rang and someone came in for bread, she sent Crystal out front. "You stay where I can see you," she said.

21

Path

"Just you and me now," said Heron when Aster was gone. She led me back into the loomhouse. "Just as much work, though. You'll have to carry the cloth yourself. Make you strong."

"I am strong," I said.

"Hah. At least you're not tired. You slept last night, didn't you? No circles under your eyes now. You'll sleep tonight, too."

She left to light the burner under the vat, and I shouldered the first bolt of undyed cloth and followed her. We repeated the work of the previous morning except that now there was only one Hand to lift and pull and heave and tug. By the time I had got the five bolts of cloth up to the platform, I was tired and sore. But there was no time to rest, only one thing after another. With two doing the work of three, there was no easy rhythm to the work, just the need to keep moving and think ahead. And I knew this was what Heron wanted. There was no reason for her to have sent Aster away that morning. We could have brought all the cloth to the Circle the next day. No, Heron wanted me to herself, and she wanted me tired and hot and off balance.

"You did this on purpose, didn't you?" I asked.

"Did what?"

"Sent Aster off by herself. So you would be with me alone."

"Excellent. You are paying attention and thinking. Yes, you are right. I chose this."

"Why?"

"You are here to learn. From being my Hand. A Hand I can use. A Hand I can train. When I pick a Hand, I take care. I choose well. From knowledge."

"What knowledge?"

"Knowledge of you, girl."

"Me?"

"Yes," she said. "I know everything about you. About that father of yours, that Ram. A man who thinks he is a sheep. Now I know something about sheep, too."

I stopped stirring and stared at her. "Why are you telling me this?"

"So that you will know your place. And mine." She took the paddle from me, roughly, and stirred the cloth hard. "Don't think you can slack off because I'm talking to you. Now is the time to listen and learn, but you will not stop work while you listen." She gave the paddle back to me, and I plunged it into the hot dye.

"What I know of sheep," said Heron, "is that you lead one and they all follow. So I led that Ram, your father. I knew he had an eye for pretty fluff. Him taking that dancer for your mother told me that."

My mother. She was talking about my mother. "Did you know her?" I asked.

"I didn't need to. People tell me things. They told me enough about her to let me know that Ram was a man who could be led by pretty things. So I led him. Led him to give me you."

"What do you mean?"

"I gave him cloth, pretty cloth. Told him you were worth that much to me to take for a Hand. And he was glad to let you come to me."

"But I thought you took me because I was good. Good with the cloth."

"Girl, listen. You are good. You are the best I have seen. I would not have wasted cloth on Ram if you were not."

I nodded, still stirring. The fumes and steam from the dye put tears in my eyes, and the burner roared in my ears.

"But I wanted something from your father, see? I wanted

wool. And I led him, that sheep of a man, to give it to me. When your time as Hand is done, he will give me the wool from more sheep than I can count. Because he will believe you have become valuable to him. I led the big sheep, and the herd followed. Came to me. All for some pretty cloth."

"You traded for me."

"Of course, girl. I traded for you. Showed him what you were worth. You thank me for that. If someone had showed my mother what I was worth when I was young, I would be twice what I am now. Twice!" She slammed her staff into the platform as she said the words, so hard that the whole vat boomed. By this time I had worked the last bolt of cloth into the dye. Soon it would be boiling, hot enough for the fixer to go in.

"Knowledge," she said. "Before you came here I knew all about you. Your father, your mother, too. Just a couple of animals, that Ram and Cat. I knew what she did with you, the little fool. How she took you away for a year and brought you back, left you at the fire for your father."

"But who knew? Who told you?"

"Your aunties, girl. They were falling all over themselves to tell me that story." For the first time I heard her laugh. It made me cold, despite the heat rising from the burner beneath my feet. I clutched my mother's pendant.

"Yes, what you have from your mother. I know that, too."

I had been handed off, from my mother to my father,

and now to Heron. A thing. A Hand. Hand me away. I wanted out. Out. But there was nowhere to go. Except into the vat. And that would do it, I knew. I would not be Heron's then.

"So I am a thing, I am cloth, a sheep, a Hand to you. You learn about me, you trade for me. Like a sheep. But not this sheep. Not now." I would leap into the vat of dye rather than stay with her. She was not strong like my father. There would be no powerful arms to keep me from the fire this time. I knew how to jump. My legs had taken me from rock to branch, made leaps none of my cousins could follow. No one would follow me now.

I tensed in the rising steam, felt my feet firm on hot wood, and found my purchase.

She saw. "You will not do this," she said.

"Then you stop me, old woman," I cried.

And she did.

She swung her staff with both hands like an ax and broke my leg even as I was starting to jump. I fell off the platform to the ground, saw the end of the broken bone push through my skin, and fainted.

22

Bird

I felt Ma's eyes on me the whole time we worked. The bell would ring and Crystal would go to the front room to take care of whoever it was. I tried to look through the door to see if it might be Aster. But I never saw her. Whenever I could, between setting loaves in the ovens and taking them out, I would try to look out the window toward the Weavers' Yard, hoping to catch a glimpse of Aster or even Path and Heron busy at work. I didn't see them, must have missed Aster coming back from the Circle with her empty cart. I almost missed the Vultures.

"Bird, will you stop staring over there and get back to work?" called Ma.

I was standing with my arms up to the elbows in dough in our big bowl, looking out the window. I don't know how long I had been standing there without moving.

"He's tired, Ma," said Crystal.

"Tired. I know what makes him tired. He should have thought of that before. Bird!" she called again. "Move now, or that dough will stick to your arms, and we'll have to bake you, too."

And then, out of the corner of my eye, I saw them turning in to the Weavers' Yard. They had passed the bakery while I was looking at Ma. Two figures in dark brown robes, hoods pulled over their heads. They walked slowly, Sun Came and Spark, but no longer Sun Came and Spark. Now they wore their Vulture robes, and that meant only one thing. Someone had died, and they were coming to do what Vulture does. Vulture comes to take you when you must go. When it is time. I froze and remembered Walset coming to me in the night, repeating Path's name. Cats knew, sometimes, when a person they liked was in danger. And they would speak. If I had paid attention . . .

I pulled my arms from the dough and ran out of the bakery, scraping the sticky stuff off me as I went. I could hear Ma and Crystal calling me back, but it didn't matter. I ran on, into the Weavers' Yard, blindly going from tent to tent until I heard voices. And then I did what no one should ever do. I pushed open the tent flap and ran inside, to where Spark and Sun Came as Vulture were tending the dead. The room was dim. I saw the fire, heard the rattles and the chant, smelled the smoke of the herbs they used, and saw the body on the floor. It was purple with dye, the way Path's face had been just weeks ago. But it was not Path. It was Heron. Then I looked up and saw what you must see only once. Vulture's face. Spark and Sun Came were wearing their masks, a sight only the dead or another Vulture should see. The masks were gold, solid gold, for all I could tell, with great hooked beaks and eyes of emerald. I should not have seen this, I thought, and knelt on the floor, frightened. One of them threw a handful of powder on the fire, which made a thick smoke. I breathed the smoke and fell asleep.

I dreamed I dived into a dark pool, straight to the bottom, and dug through the mud until I had made a tunnel. I pulled myself along until the tunnel started to pull me, as if it were the gullet of some beast. Finally it spat me out in a forest. I touched the trunk of the nearest tree and climbed onto a low branch. The next thing I knew, the low branch was high in the air, higher than all the other trees in the forest. I stepped off the branch and flew. My arms, hands, and fingers were long wings, wings so big that I barely had to move them as my body tilted from side to side in the air, which was full of smoke from a big fire somewhere. I was not alone. Spark and Sun Came were with me too, and Heron. I was a bird with them. We flew higher and higher, circling in the air rising from the fire, and watched Heron rise with us. She looked like herself but younger. And at peace. We rose with the smoke until we were so high that all the earth was a tiny speck below. The rising smoke made a flat cloud, and I could see each particle of it, round and wrinkly like peppercorns. Heron touched one of the particles and disappeared inside. I thought I heard a monkey's cry, and then everything was black.

When I woke, I was lying on the tent floor. I looked up at Spark and Sun Came, seeing their human faces. They looked very serious but not angry.

"You are one of us now," Spark said. "You have climbed the Tree of the World. And found the only way down."

I thought about what I had seen in my dream. "But that was a dream."

"No. And yes. It is a place you can go if the bird calls you."

They helped me up. The room spun around me as I tried to stand. I almost fell but they caught me.

"You have to use your legs now," said Spark. "You're back on the ground."

I looked down, saw my feet on the tent floor. But I could still feel what it was like to ride the rising air. I held out my hands, which had carried me like wings, touched each finger.

"It will never leave you," said Spark. "But you will get used to it."

"What do you mean?"

"I told you. You are one of us now."

"You are a Vulture, Bird," said Sun Came. "You will wear the robe and walk with us on Midsummer Day. And over the next year we will teach and you will learn. And the mask that is Spark's will be yours."

"Vulture called and you came," said Spark. "I am an old man. The gift moves."

"It moves," I said, full of wonder at all that had passed to me. Then I remembered Path. "But what about Path? What happened to her?"

"She has a broken leg," said Sun Came. "And she's asleep. Maybe Aster will let you see her. We have to talk to Aster anyway. Time to get you a robe." They helped me from the tent, my legs all wobbly. The body lay on the floor, clay now. Heron was gone.

Aster was in the loomhouse. Her eyes were red from tears. She stood when we came in, surprised to see me with Spark and Sun Came.

"Bird. Why are you here?"

"The bird called him," said Spark. "And now he needs a robe."

"A Vulture robe," she said.

"Yes."

"Because he saw you."

"Because he saw us and came with us. And Heron," said Sun Came.

She looked at me. "You saw that?"

I nodded. "Aster, how is Path?" I had to know.

"She is all right. But her leg is broken."

"What happened?"

"I don't know. When I came back from the Circle, there was nobody here. Then I heard the burner under the big vat. It was going full blast. I went over there and found Path on the ground, with her leg badly broken. I could see the bone and there was blood, so I ran for Snake and brought him back here as fast as I could. He set Path's leg, and we got Heron out of the vat after it cooled down. Something happened between them. I don't know what."

"Can I see Path?"

"For a minute, I guess. Snake gave her something to make her sleep so he could fix her leg."

She led us out to their tent and showed us in. Path lay on her back on her mat, pale and sleeping. Her right leg was in a cast. I was relieved to see her, to know that she would be all right.

"You should leave now," Aster said. "I will make your robe, and you can come over and try it on tomorrow. She will be awake by then."

Still in their robes, Spark and Sun Came took me home. It was not an easy trip because I felt like I was still flying and had forgotten how to walk. They had to half carry me, and I stumbled with them through our gate and into the bakery. The sight of them with me silenced whatever protests Ma was going to make. Vulture business was serious, and when it came your way, you dropped everything. Even baking for Midsummer Day.

We sat around the table.

"This is one of the ways Vulture calls a person," said Spark. "When someone comes upon us at our work and sees. It is the surest way to be called, and the bird has called your boy. He is young, but the gift is his. I am old and have been waiting for someone like Bird to come."

Ma said, "Does he have to go away?"

"No," said Sun Came. "We will teach him over the next year or so, and he will be ready to take Spark's place. We do ask that he wear the robe and walk with us to the fire, with all the Years."

Spark said, "When there is a new one of us, we want people to know. To see that this gift is passing among us."

"Aster said she would make him a robe for tomorrow. And Path may help if she feels up to it."

Spark looked at me. I looked back, still not right in my head from what had happened in the tent. Somewhere inside, a part of me was flying, long brown wings soaring into whatever world we go to next. The part of me that was sitting in the bakery heard Spark's words.

"So. Bird Speaks, the bird speaks in you right enough. And speaks still. You are still on the wing somewhere, aren't you?"

I nodded.

"You are not as you were, Bird. You have come through

the door that goes between worlds. The way is in you, and you will carry it with you always. On Midsummer Day you will wear your robe. You will be Vulture, like us. People will not see Bird the baker. They will not see the boy who made bread, who laughed with their children, who ran in the sea. They will see the big brown bird who knows the way in and out, who will come for them when it is their time. They will look at you and see their own end. You will see this in their eyes."

"Will they still know me?"

"Oh, yes," Sun Came said. "But it will take a while to get used to. For them and you, both. The day after tomorrow the year turns from Vulture to Wheat. The seed in the ground dies to live again."

They both stood up and looked at me, serious, calm. Spark spoke. "You have started down a long path, Bird. As long as time. But it will begin with Midsummer Day."

And they left. Ma said, "Bird. Vulture. Just into your second Turn, and you are a Year at Midsummer." She shook her head, then glared at Crystal and me. "Let's see if we can get a little baking done before tomorrow."

We set to work together in the familiar way, and I remembered what Spark had said. In two days the year of Wheat would begin. As I worked, I thought of flour and its passage to dough. Pull, shape, pat, set on the sheet to go in the oven, do it again. The dough soft in my fingers, alive, breathing its slow yeasty breath. I follow the gift back to the soil and think of the wind that blew over the field where this grain grew, the sun that warmed it, the dirt from which its roots drew life. I see this life passing through my fingers into one hungry mouth after another, mine included. From sun to seed to dirt to rain to mill to table, the gift must move. It is life itself. *Let my life turn with the year, then. Let me be seed in the ground,* I thought.

When the sun was down, Ma decided that we were done.

"It is enough. It is more than enough. We will stop now and we can rest. That is a proper gift for us all."

23

Path

I did not wake until the next day. The day before Midsummer Day. I opened my eyes and found I was in the tent, on my own mat, soft blankets around me. Aster was there. At first I was confused, thinking that the next world looked an awful lot like the one I had just left. Then it came back to me. I looked down at my leg, remembering Heron breaking it with her staff before I fell to the ground.

Aster came in. "You are awake," she said. "I thought you were going to sleep forever. Snake came and set your leg, Path. But it was a bad break, and he had to give you something to put you to sleep so he could fix it. It worked."

"Heron will be furious with me," I said. "I don't know what she'll do now. I don't know if I can stay anymore, not after what I said to her."

There was silence.

"Path. Heron is dead. I found her in the big vat. When I came back from the Circle, I couldn't find anybody and went looking. I heard the burner and found you on the ground by the vat with your leg broken. Heron was in the vat. Her staff was broken in two."

"She hit me with it. I was going to . . . I was going to jump in the dye myself. End everything. I dared her to stop me."

"It looks like she did," said Aster.

"She must have fallen in when she hit me, lost her balance and couldn't catch herself."

"I think so," said Aster. "Then the Vultures came for Heron, and then Bird came, too. He ran into the tent while they were carrying her spirit away. He thought they had come for you. He stayed there with them the whole time, and they came out with him and took him back to the bakery."

"What do you suppose that means?"

"He is a Vulture now. We have to make a robe for him so he can walk with the Years tomorrow."

Bird a Vulture. Because of me. He saw the Vultures with Heron because he thought it was me in there who was dead. Aster left to get the things for Bird's robe.

I lay back on the blankets, my leg sore. I wondered what would happen with Heron gone.

Aster returned with the soft brown cloth, scissors, needles, and thread and set to work. I had to sit and watch as she cut the cloth. I wasn't strong enough to help with that. But I could sew when it was time. For a while we were quiet together, the only sound in the tent the whoosh of the cloth as Aster pulled it to and fro and the snick of the scissors as she cut the pieces to make the robe.

Finally Aster spoke. "Path. You don't have to tell me, but I want to know what happened."

"What happened?"

"With you and Heron. I know she sent me off to the Circle because she wanted to be alone with you. Why? What did she do?"

I took a deep breath and told her. When I had finished, she was silent for a long time. The half-made robe lay between us.

"In the end she saved your life," Aster said. "You were special to her. It made me jealous when she would talk about you before you even got here. Because you're so young and you were her favorite. But she was right. You are as good as she said."

"She just pushed," I said. "She didn't show any affection, didn't give me anything but the work."

"She didn't give affection to herself, either."

"No, she didn't. Just the cloth. Fabric and color."

"And that's not enough," Aster said. "Not for you or me or anybody. Even her."

I looked down at the cloth cut for Bird's robe, deep brown and shaped like a person, like a skin. *Heron*, I thought. She lay between us with this cloth. When we took it up to sew its seams, we would be taking up her gift of art and work, too. And she would live in us.

"Let's finish this, then," I said.

The Vulture robe is an unusual garment. It covers the wearer from the top of the head to the toes and must show no seam. And it has several deep pockets for things Vultures carry with them, their herbs and rattles and feathers. It was hard to make, and we had to guess at Bird's size, though I had a pretty good idea of how big he was. I could close my eyes and see him in front of me, touch his shoulders and chest with my mind. When we had done all we could do, it was time to get Bird for the final fitting.

"I'll go get him," said Aster.

She returned with Bird a few minutes later.

"Path," he said.

"Bird."

"When I saw you last you were asleep and they had just fixed your leg. Do you feel all right?"

"I'm sore, Bird. And I am a fool. A fool for running away from you. You who cared for me."

"I am so glad to see you, Path. I am so glad. Happy. I

am . . ." Then he bent down and kissed my cheek. "This, for you my gift."

"It moves," I said. "And this, for you." His robe was lying on my legs. Aster gathered it up and held it against him. It looked right.

"Come now, you'll have to try it on so we can fit you," she said. He slipped it over his head, Aster helping so the stitches would hold. He looked a little uneasy when he finally got into it. But the robe looked fine on him. Aster pinned up the hem, made adjustments in the shoulder seams, and helped him get it off.

"I'll have to practice getting into that," he said.

"Getting out of it is what you'll have to practice," said Aster. "When you take that off tomorrow at the fire, every eye in town will be on you."

"I know," he said. He held the robe, running his fingers over the soft brown cloth. He stood like that for a long time, just trying to take it all in, I guess. Then he handed the robe to Aster.

"Here. Thank you."

"We'll have it ready for you in the morning," she said.

Bird turned to me. "I am sorry about Heron. But I am so glad to see you. To see you are all right. Will you come to the Circle with us tomorrow?"

Midsummer Day. I wouldn't have to go, not with my leg broken. "I can't walk, Bird."

"I will push you. You can be with Aster at the weavers' stall. You won't need to walk to do that."

"He's right," said Aster. "There will be a lot for us to do tomorrow. You can help. And you need to be there. For the fire. For the year to turn."

So it was decided for me. I would go to the fire for the first time since my mother had left me.

"All right. I'll go."

"I'll see you in the morning, then," said Bird. And he was out the door.

We took up the brown cloth, making strong invisible stitches to hold the robe together. When we finished, there were no seams you could see. It was the best work we knew how to do. Before tomorrow was over it would be ashes.

24

Bird

I was up before dawn on Midsummer Day. The bakery was quiet, the ovens cold. Today there would be no baking, no mixing of flour and yeast and water. No running with hot pans of bread from the oven to the cooling racks. Today we would take the last of our work to the Circle, set it out in our stall, and wait for things to begin. But for a little while in the dark, before everything got going, I could be alone. I touched all the familiar things: the pans and spoons and cups and paddles, the bins of flour and sugar and yeast—all empty now. You use up everything for Midsummer Day. And I had used up something in myself, too. Used it up when I rushed into the tent looking for Path and found Spark and

Sun Came with Heron. I had used up the thing that had been pushing me out of the bakery all this year. I held my hands up in front of my face, ghostly fingers in the first light. Fingers in the flour. Feathers in the air. I would walk between them from now on.

I went through the door and into the backyard.

"Bird. Bird." Walset shoved his head into my ankles, then circled around my feet, waiting for me to pick him up. I laid him on my shoulder like a warm sack of flour and listened to his purr.

"Waiting for food, aren't you?"

"Fish," he said and jumped down.

I took him inside, found a piece of fish, put it in his dish, and filled his bowl with water. I could hear Ma and Crystal moving around upstairs, so I put on the kettle to boil.

Fixing tea, I got us some rolls from the big pile we would take to the Circle. Ma and Crystal came downstairs. Ma looked around the bakery, eyes taking inventory of clean counters, pans and tools in their places. Satisfied, she sat down at the table.

"Well," she said, "I think we are ready. Crystal, Bird, you have both done well." She poured herself some tea and motioned for us to sit with her. She picked up a roll, broke it in half, and ate. "What we have baked this week is very good." She chewed some more. "Very good. And you both made it so."

Crystal and I waited.

"Bird," she said, "I had been worried about you. Worried about your restlessness, about your wandering mind and heart and where they would lead you. Your father has been worried too. We've been concerned about your becoming so fascinated with that weaver girl, Path, and where that would take you. But I see that meeting her was part of your own way. Path. A name with some meaning for you now. You walk into a new part of your life, your own path, this day, and that girl is part of what called you there."

Ma had never talked to me like this before.

"You go on now," she continued. "Go to the weavers and get your robe. And your friend. We'll wait for you."

"All right, Ma," I said. "I'll go." I left the bakery, feeling things slip and move inside me. I would come back in a few minutes, but I wouldn't be the same person. My life was turning with the year. I found Path and Aster in their tent. Path still lay on her mat, but she looked much better than she had the day before.

"Here, Bird. This is your robe." She held it up for me, and I took it and let it fall over my head, feeling the weight of what I would do land on my shoulders with the cloth.

Path and Aster just looked at me for a minute, and I felt their gaze as Bird Speaks and Vulture both. The first piece of my new life.

"Well," I said, running my hands over the robe, "it is wonderful. I thank you."

"The gift moves," said Aster and Path together.

"It moves."

And it was time to go. Snake had left a wheelchair for Path, with fat tires that would roll over the sand. "Aster and I can lift you onto the wheelchair, Path. We need to get to the Circle."

"No, really, I don't have to go," she said.

"Yes, you do," I said. "Everybody goes."

We lifted Path under her shoulders and hips and carried her to the chair. I was surprised at how light she was. No wonder she could climb trees like a monkey.

We stopped at the bakery for Ma and Crystal, and they each came out with sacks of rolls and sweets, the last baking. They each carried two, gave one sack to Aster and put one in Path's lap.

"Be careful now," said Ma. "Don't hurt that leg." She must have decided she liked Path a little better, I thought. She fussed over the pillows and cushions after setting the sack of rolls back on Path's lap.

"You're all right? You're comfortable? You don't hurt, do you?"

"No. Really, I'm fine," said Path.

And off we went. A real parade we were, with Ma and Crystal and Aster followed by a Vulture pushing a weaver on a wheelchair. When people got close enough to see that the Vulture was me, they just stared, silent. I felt their eyes on me.

Path was quiet during the whole trip. When we were almost there, I said to her, "And this will be the first time you've gone to the fire since your mother left you?"

"Yes," she said. "It is. I always hid. They tried to find me every time, but they never did."

I could believe that. "You knew how to hide."

"Yes, I did."

The trees opened up by the road, and suddenly we were at the Circle, morning sunlight pink on the stalls. A few people were there already, though the big crowd was several hours off. I followed Aster to the weavers' stall, and she helped me roll Path behind the counter.

"I'll see you soon," I said to Path. "I need to find Spark and Sun Came."

"All right," said Path. "Bird," she called as I was walking away, "you look good in your robe."

"Thanks to you," I said. I walked across the Circle, searching for brown robes like mine. Everything was quiet and ready around me, a big field that would fill with a thousand wild people in a few hours.

25

Path

I didn't want to be there. I watched Bird walk off across the Circle and cursed my broken leg. I'd trusted my feet and wits to keep me away from the fire ever since my mother had brought me back to Boon, but I could not trust my feet now. They had been taken from me until my leg healed.

I looked around. Aster was busy pulling cloth from boxes, arranging scarves, dresses, all sorts of clothing and banners, and streamers of bright cloth on the tables placed at the front of the stall. Most of it was new to me. She and Heron had been busy for months before I came to the Weavers' Yard.

"What can I do?" I asked.

"Nothing now," said Aster. "But later there will be plenty to do. You can hand out things to people who come by the stall. Toward the end of the day there will be a big rush. They'll empty us out an hour before the fire starts."

"And what do we do then?"

"Sit and watch. There's nothing like it."

"Why? It's just Midsummer Day. The same thing every year."

"I don't know," said Aster. "It's different from the way they do it in Lanta. In the city there are too many people to have one Circle, one fire. So there are many, all over the place. There would be a big parade for everybody to see, and all the Years would walk past. Then we'd go home and have a small Circle and fire with everybody in the building where we lived. And we knew that all over town people were doing the same thing. So we were all together in that way. But here there is one Circle for everybody. And that's different. What was it like for you, in Boon?"

What I had seen so far wasn't so different from what I remembered. "We'd come down from the pasture to the Circle. It was in the New River bottom, in a big bend, and we would be there all day. The Circle was about the same size, too, and full of people and stalls and food and shouting. About like this." Except, of course, that I wasn't there. I was hiding far away up the mountain, high in a tree. Far enough away so that I could hear no music, no voices, and see no glow of the fire. So this would be a new experience for me, familiar as it was.

The Circle was starting to fill up now, and cooking smells were in the air, with bits of music floating past. People began to come to our stall, fingering the cloth and clothing. They would ask about my leg and have a word or two about Heron. And after a while they began to pick up our wares and put them on. I watched our cloth slowly disappear from the tables, only to reappear in the crowd as a flash of orange here, green stripes there, a blue scarf and yellow streamers flying in the air. It reminded me of my first sight of the Banks from the boat.

Every so often one or another of the Years would walk past. This was the only day of the year when you could see them all in their robes, and they had to move around so that everyone could see them. I watched Ant pass in his black robe, Bear in dark brown, and Sun and Moon wearing the cloth I had brought to Sun Came two weeks earlier. And then two of them came to the stall. One was Snake, whose robe was a complicated twill woven to look like scales. The other was Sun Came in her Vulture robe. I didn't recognize her at first.

"How's that leg?" asked Snake.

"All right," I said. "It still hurts."

"It was a bad break," he said. "So be careful. It should heal fine if you take care of it. I'll come in a week to take a look at it." He left, disappearing into the crowd.

"Path," Sun Came said, "I know you can't get around, so I've brought you some food. You need to eat."

She put a plate in front of me, with some of Bird's bread, along with corn, greens, fried fish, and two round fried things with sauce.

"The gift moves," she said.

"It moves," I said and ate. The round fried things were wonderful. "What are these?" I asked.

"Crab cakes," she said.

"So you can eat crab?"

"All the time," she said. She watched me eat.

"You know," she said, "the year turns today. Turns from Vulture to Wheat. From the bird to the seed in the ground." She looked at me hard. "Let it turn in you, Path. Make a place for the seed. You know it's time."

"I don't know if there's any room in me at all," I said.

"Then you need to make some. And this is the time and place to make it."

"With what?" I asked.

"The time will come, and you will know what to do." She squeezed my hand and left.

From then on, everything went faster. Our work kept melting into the crowds as Aster put out more and more cloth and clothes until all the boxes were empty. Crystal came by, her headscarf bright on her head, and asked if I was all right. She was with a tall man I recognized from Battery House. They laughed as they left and ran into the trees. Soon our tables were empty, and everything began to get loud. People ran and shouted, some of them in groups of ten or twenty, all holding one of our banners. They'd run as fast as they could, trip on the cloth, fall down, get up, and do it again, shouting and laughing. Bird came and brought Aster and me mugs of beer.

"Here. You should at least taste it," he said.

"Thank you, Bird," said Aster and drank hers down.

"All right," I said and drank some of mine. But it was bitter and fizzy. I didn't like it much. "Ugh," I said, "it's not for me."

"It's wheat beer. They make it only for Wheat year," said Aster, "and you've had your taste."

"I saw Crystal with a man," I said. "From Battery House, I think."

"Yes, that's Bright," said Bird. "She's had her eye on him for a long time. Finally he's starting to pay attention."

"He ought to," I said.

Just then Spider appeared out of the crowd. Tall, bearded, wearing the shiny black-and-yellow spider robe, he came up behind Bird and put his hands over Bird's eyes. *What is going on*, I wondered.

"Who is it?" he asked Bird.

"Does he have eight legs?" Bird asked. "Does he speak? Does he spin?"

Spider took his hands off Bird's eyes.

"Path," said Bird, "this is my father. And Spider also."

"I am How the Wind Goes," he said. "The gift moves."

"It moves. And I am Path Down the Mountain. The gift moves."

"It moves," he said. "And Bird here. His robe is so shabby, his wings so small, he will never fly, never at all."

"But it's not," I said. "His robe is fine and new. We just made it. And he's a Vulture now." What was he talking about? Why insult his own son?

Bird and his father were laughing.

"Path," said Bird, "my father comes from people who talk backward when something is important. So he means the opposite of what he says."

"I mean that I am very proud of my son," he said.

"It's about time for the fire," said Bird. "And I have to go. I have to walk around where people can see me. Like the other Years. I'll see you at the fire."

"See you," I said and watched him lope away.

His father turned to me. "Bird is lucky to know you. Lucky indeed. And I'm talking forward this time." He smiled at me and disappeared into the throng.

All around, everyone was shouting, and then I saw light from the center of the Circle. The fire was lit. Aster pushed my wheelchair out of the stall.

"Got to get you out of here."

"Why?" I asked.

"You'll see," she said.

People were running past us to the fire. And then two

men picked up one of our tables and took it with them. And more people picked up the other tables, and all at once a whole crowd of people began to pull on the wood of the stall and tear it down. In a minute it was gone, the ground bare where it had stood.

"That's why," said Aster. "You didn't need to be in there with your broken leg and the whole stall coming apart around you."

"No, I didn't." The same thing was happening all around us. There were sounds of boards breaking, nails being pulled loose, and crazy shouting and laughter as everything that had been built for Midsummer Day came down at once. It had taken weeks to build all of it, but it seemed to come down in minutes. When most of the crowd had passed us on their way to the fire, Aster began to push me in their wake.

"It's better to let them go first," she said. "That way we'll have more room."

Up ahead the fire was bright, hot. As we got close, I could hear its sound—a dull roar mixed with the crackles and pops and bangs of burning lumber. People ran to the edge of the pit, pulled off their clothes, and threw them into the fire. They sprinted away naked, skin bright in the hot light. Now the fire was making a wind, pulling air into the Circle to feed the flames.

"Here I go," Aster said. She ran up to the edge of the pit, pulled her blue shift over her head, and gave it to the fire.

She ran back to me, flushed. Then Crystal was there. And Bird.

"Path," he said, "you are at the fire at last."

"Yes."

"Then you know what to do." Bird and Crystal took hold of the chair and pushed it closer to the flames, which were hot on our faces. The wind roared in my ears, louder than the shouting voices of the people around us. Crystal stepped out of her tunic, threw it into the fire, and then took off the headscarf I had made for her. I watched it float into the flames. Bird reached into the big pocket of his robe and brought out the birdman he had made and I had painted. He smiled at me and sent it into the fire. His robe followed, a long dark shadow that hung in the brightness before it disappeared. Then he took hold of the wheelchair.

"Now you," he said.

He pushed me closer to the pit. It was the day my mother had left me. The day that had never ended for me. But Sun Came was right. The time had come and I knew what to do. I slipped off my shift and threw it in. The flames took it, and then I was naked except for my mother's pendant. I pulled the Sun and Moon over my head and held it in my hand. I felt my mother's hands holding me as she danced, heard her laugh, and saw her dance away from me at the fire in Boon. I looked at the Sun and Moon one last time, saw the light and dark, night and day. Then I threw it as hard as I could into the fire. It shone against the night for a moment, and then it was gone. Forever.

Something came loose in me. The years moving, time starting up again. Then came the tears. All the tears I would not cry for my mother, coming all at once. I could feel someone pushing the chair away from the fire. It was Bird.

"Path, are you all right?" he asked.

I couldn't speak. I sobbed and shook for a long time until there were no more tears left. When I opened my eyes, they were all there. Bird, Crystal, their ma, Aster, and their father, who looked awfully bony without the spider robe. They were all quiet, tired. Around us were faces in the firelight as far as I could see. A thousand of us, each one empty and naked at the turning of the year.

After a while people began to leave the Circle in little groups. Everyone was very quiet, soft voices above the pops and snaps of the dying fire. I could hear the ocean again. Bird and I stayed until the fire was just glowing lumps in the dark. By then his ma and father and Crystal were gone. Aster, too.

Bird pushed me back down the road to the bakery and Weavers' Yard. I touched my chest where my mother's Sun and Moon had hung. "I can't believe it's gone," I said. "I had it for so long." I could feel its familiar weight still. "But I took it, you know. It was never a gift."

"You were just a little girl," said Bird. "You did what you could."

"And stayed a little girl," I said, and then I cried some more, tears finding their way up from places I thought must be dry by now. Bird kept pushing me down the dark road. He stopped when we got to the bakery. It was an hour or two before sunup. Walset jumped on top of me. "Path," he said and started to knead my stomach with his front paws, claws and all. "Ouch," I said. "Stop, Walset." I picked him up and held him. "What happens now?" I asked Bird.

"We'll sleep a lot and wake up with headaches and singed eyebrows. We'll walk around in a fog."

"But what do we do? Do you start baking, start life again?"

"Life doesn't stop," he said, "but we can't start baking because there's no more flour."

"No flour?"

"Of course not. We used it all. You have to use everything on Midsummer Day."

"But what do you eat?"

"Nothing. You get hungry. Empty inside. And you know that hunger is good. Because you feel an empty place in you, waiting."

"And then what?"

He laughed. "When we get hungry enough, I'll teach you how to fish."

* * *

I did learn to fish, sitting in a chair on the beach, with a long pole in my hands. After a week, bags of flour, yeast, and sugar and tins of oil appeared at the bakery door, left there by Wheat in the middle of the night. With that, the Midsummer Day festival was over, and life at the bakery resumed its normal pace. I lived there with Bird and Crystal and their ma until I could walk again. Then I went back to the Weavers' Yard with Aster. In the last year we've made cloth as good as anything Heron ever wove, though not so much of it. The seed that sprouted in me when I gave away the Sun and Moon has grown, and I still find tears to water it. In a few days the year will turn from Wheat to Sun, and I will go to the fire again. All these things are Heron's gifts to me. I try to let them flow in everything I weave. Her last gift, my broken leg, healed good as new. I can still outrun Bird. Sometimes, though, I let him catch me. The gift moves.

ACKNOWLEDGMENTS

Thanks to George Ella, Benn, and Joey for their help, presence, and bright spirits.

I thank readers of earlier drafts of this novel, especially Dick Jackson, Jenny Davis, Leatha Kendrick, Jim Tomlinson, and Kendra Marcus. Many thanks to Silas House and all the Housewriters: Beth Dotson Brown, Cynthia Cain, Barbara Fischer, Shelda Hale, Jim Tomlinson, and Jean Welch. Your words and friendship helped make this book what it is. Jerrie Oughton's perceptive commentary helped turn it into something readable.

Lewis Hyde's remarkable book *The Gift: Imagination and the Erotic Life of Property* showed me what it could be like to live in a gift-based culture.

I thank Dobree Adams and Harriet Giles, weavers who opened their workshops to me and let me spend some time with their art and craft and tools.

Finally, thanks to Dalia Geffen for copyediting, and especially to Margaret Raymo at Houghton Mifflin for bringing this story to print.